Trail

to

Justice

a short novel
by
C. Lowry
and
P. LaVelle Muhr

Trail to Justice is a work of fiction. Any similarity to persons alive or dead is unintentional and coincidental. Geographical features and distances between or among sites may be greatly distorted, as are traits and actions of the characters presented.

Copyright 2023

ISBN # 979-8-9864581-7-5

Published in North Carolina by the authors

For further information or to order copies of Trail to Justice, please email
clowry@carolina.rr.com
or
pjmuhr@gmail.com

Dedicated to
Oldtimers of the Old West
and
the slightly younger Class of '58

Trail

to

Justice

Chapter 1

He rode across the prairie from the southeast on a sweated-up sorrel, a lame dog bobbing along behind him. All three--cowboy, horse, dog--looked grim and dirty; all three eyed the landscape carefully. The wind had died down a little, but it was a bit cooler. They'd run into cold air tonight, but it would be hot again tomorrow. The cowboy pulled a piece of jerked beef from his shirt pocket, bit off a mouthful, then tossed the rest back to the dog. The horse would have to wait until evening to graze on whatever they might be lucky enough to find along the river. They moved mostly across grassland, but often the river twisted into view--muddy and swift-moving. No boats or barges; no homesteads. Game seemed scarce: a couple of cottontails, a few prairie chickens. He didn't want to shoot, anyway, so it made no difference.

The cowboy was tall and lean, the sorrel stocky, the dog way too thin. They were leaving a place of comfort and grief, headed for paybacks and maybe even some peace of mind. They carried all their needs--physical and mental-- with them. They'd traveled far and had only a short way to go before they'd know their chances of success. The cowboy counted on his horse and his dog; the dependence was mutual.

The saddle creaked in a rhythmic accompaniment to the quiet footfalls of the sorrel as the trio moved slightly to the south. The sun was lowering and the cowboy was glad for the brim of his hat to shade his eyes. He looked ahead toward the horizon. Perhaps a stand of trees there in the distance, a slight rise in the prairie---maybe a quiet gully for a rest. He checked his Winchester, chunking it gently in the scabbard, then patted one saddle bag to feel shells. He wouldn't take a chance on meeting up with anyone without being sure he could fend for the three of them.

An hour later, they could see the trees clearly, make out hills and gully, sense a familiar smell: the river again. They would stop to water and rest, then move on toward what might reveal a town, probably a half a night's ride. They'd go on in the dark this time, try to make it to the first stop on the revenge ride.

"We'll stop here, guys," he grunted. He didn't usually talk to either horse or dog unless it was an emergency or to beckon them, but the possibility of rest and water warranted the brief comment. He loosened the cinch on the sorrel and followed the dog to the edge of the river. Water too muddy for the canteen. Walked a bit upstream and located a small creek flowing into the river. Filled canteen, drank slowly and gratefully, topped off canteen, led the sorrel back to the small patch of prairie grass beneath the trees. He took the bridle off, got the Winchester from the scabbard, then sat on the ground, stretching his legs out before him. He tipped his hat lower, leaned back on the sturdy tree, and closed his eyes for a brief rest. Like always, closed eyes meant opened memories. Images of the ramshackle house and barn, the quiet little kitchen, the corral newly repaired. And then the vision of Sullie, blonde hair lifted by the wind, brow inquisitive as she gazed toward him. Then pain, instant and huge, and her eyes startled wider, blood came from everywhere, and Sullie fell sideways, no sound from her at all. The sound of the shot came almost immediately, and it echoed once between the buildings. Then silence, and he struggled to move, to get close to her, to save her, to bring her back, to change it all, to undo it. It was the same every time. His legs wouldn't work right, his arms flailed, his voice wouldn't come out except in short grunts. Sullie. Sullie.

Chapter 2

He did what he always did when the bad memories came: He commanded his mind to bring up the good images. He saw again Sullie at the ranch, then earlier, at her dad's place. The Marshes had moved into the old Brackett place, a big ranch with good pasture, plenty of water. He heard in town that Marsh was looking for a hand to break horses. When he rode up to the main house, he got a glimpse first of Marsh, then of a shadowed blue figure behind the front door. He dismounted and approached old Marsh.

"Hi, sir. I'm Brady Quillan, next place over." Marsh stepped forward and extended a hand.

"Hello, young man. What can I do for you?"

"Heard you were looking for help with horses. Thought maybe I could talk to you about that."

"Yeah. Well, I got a few pretty raw young horses. Need 'em ready for cattle work in a few weeks. Would you like to take a look at 'em?"

They walked toward a large corral where probably a dozen horses churned up dust. Marsh was a heavy man, belly hanging over his belt. The belt was tooled and silvered. His shirt looked custom-made, his boots were fairly new, and he walked with his toes pointed out.

"I don't need these all broke yet. Some are lame, a couple in foal. I just need about half a dozen ready to work as soon as possible."

Most of the horses looked good to Brady--not bony or scarred up, only a couple visibly a little gimpy. He saw two bays and a buckskin that looked ready to start on. The buckskin seemed real interested in them but not spooked.

"Be glad to give them a start. What kinda deal are you thinking of?"

Marsh didn't hesitate. "We can go by the head. I figure you're a fair hand with horses. I heard your name in town, and you rode in on a good one, and that's the best sign I can go by. You can work as much of the day as you need, and you can take your pick of the ones to start on. We'll settle up at the end of each week. I don't want any horse hurt, and I'd like for you not to get hurt, either." Marsh grinned at that, adjusted his hat and started around the corral to allow Brady a better look at the stock.

Suddenly a voice came from behind them. "Marsh, you have company and you didn't tell us!"

Brady turned to see two women, one with a walking stick and the other...well, the other was some kind of vision. A blonde perfection in a blue shirt and trousers, boots and a smile. He whipped his hat off, bent his head slightly.

"Hello, ma'am. Miss. Brady Quillan. Talking to Mr. Marsh about...horses." His tongue wasn't working quite right. He felt like he should shut up or say something important. The sun hit the young woman's hair like gold, and she looked at him with interest. Brady wanted his brain to kick in. Fast.

Old Marsh spoke up then, explained that Brady would be starting on the young horses. Both women exclaimed with enthusiasm, and the lady with the walking stick came closer.

"Young man...Brady...I'm so glad you're here. I just don't want either Marsh or Sullie or either of her brothers to tackle these young horses. There's too much other ranch work to do to risk somebody getting hurt on them. Some of the family, I mean." She fluttered a hand. "I surely don't mean to suggest you could get hurt without our concern." She smiled, chuckled, extended the same hand.

"I'm Mrs. Marsh, and this is Sullie. Sullivan Marsh. Our daughter." The young woman came closer, too, smiled again, and nodded.

"Nice to meet you, ma'am, miss. " He turned back toward the rancher. "I'll be going, sir. And I'll be by first thing in the morning. "

It was his first sight of the most important person in his life. Her image stayed with him that evening and into the night. And he looked for her when he rode up to the Marsh ranch the next morning, but she wasn't in sight. The work with the horses went well. He started them in a small corral, doing ground work

4

with each separately, pushing them to change direction, change gaits, get accustomed to paying attention to him.

He started with the two bays and the buckskin. All three seemed responsive and intelligent, although the two bays were a little reluctant to acknowledge him as being in charge. By midmorning he was able to get a halter on each, able to run his hand down each back. He felt he'd be able to put a saddle on the next day. He went through the whole routine again with each horse before turning them out into the adjoining paddock. He looked for Marsh or another hand but didn't see anyone as he saddled his own horse to ride home. The three young horses had access to water and hay, and Brady knew Marsh would be looking in on them by early evening.

At his own place, Brady whistled for his dog, then rode through the pasture, checking cattle and fences, water holes and windbreaks, mentally checking off each critter as healthy and calm. Back at the barn, he cared for his horse, invited the dog inside, and fixed his meat and potatoes. The dog got meat and gravy and thumped his tail on the floor in appreciation. The knife and fork clanked on the metal plate as Brady ate his meal. And thought of Sullie. And wondered why she wasn't around during the morning. There was no doubt: She was the prettiest woman he'd ever seen.

* * *

Brady stirred a bit under the tree then got back into his good memories. The first week's work with Marsh's horses went well, but there was no sight of the girl or of the rest of the family until Saturday, late morning, as he prepared to leave. She came from the house and spoke quietly with a smile.

"I like how you're handling the horses, and so does Dad. They're coming along nicely."

He tipped his hat. "Yeah, they're good stock. And the ground in the corral is good."

She came closer. "I'd like to come down to the corral to watch you closer if that's okay. I'll be quiet."

"Sure. Glad to have you. No need to be quiet. They

need all the regular commotion to get used to."

"Thanks. I'll be here on Monday."

He tipped his hat again. "Good to see you again, miss."

"I'm Sullivan. Sullie."

"Yes ma'am.....Sullie." He tipped his hat yet again and turned toward the dirt road.

The sorrel had rested all morning in the paddock and was game to pick up the pace. They headed for home at an easy lope. The ride seemed short, and they went through the same routine they did every day...check pastures and fences, water and cattle. The dog came along, checking for birds and rabbits, interesting smells.

Supper was better that evening--fresh images of the beautiful girl made the meat and potatoes a feast.

Monday morning she came to the corral just after he had started on one of the bays. The horse was a little antsy after a day off, but soon settled into the easy-paced groundwork. Brady was focused on the horse, not the girl, which was his nature: Work before pleasure, even the almost magic pleasure of Sullie at the fence. He eased the bay into the center of the corral, rubbed and patted him, then picked up a saddle blanket and continued the contact. Soon he was able to lift the saddle to the bay's side, rubbed his shoulder and barrel with it, then eased it up onto his back. The bay stepped sideways but tolerated the new sensation. Brady moved the saddle a bit, forward, backward, sideways, side to side, several times and then removed it. Did the whole deal again. And again. The bay became more relaxed, turning his head only occasionally to nose the saddle. After several repetitions, Brady rubbed the bay down with a piece of an old towel and turned him into the small paddock, then turned to his audience.

She had a wide smile as she stepped up on the bottom rail of the corral fence.

"That was great! Isn't he doing well?!"

"Yep. I'll be able to get on him in a day or so." He moved back to the paddock to lead the buckskin into the small corral. "This guy will be even better, I think. He's a quick learner."

He didn't wait for her comment but quickly started the ground work.

She soon saw that he was right: The buckskin was a quick study. He moved smoothly in response to Brady's cues, turning, stopping, changing gaits. And the introduction to the saddle pad and saddle was ho-hum for him. He obviously trusted Brady totally.

The girl watched all through the session with the buckskin, then left when Brady turned him back into the paddock. He was sorry to see her go but eager to get on to the other bay. It was a good morning's work. With a good extra added attraction: Sullie.

The days passed quickly, with Sullie often at the corral fence, more relaxed about pointing out good responses, seeing only a few slip-ups, obviously excited as Brady was able to tighten the cinch, then step into a stirrup, add a little weight, step back off, repeat, repeat, repeat. Finally, Brady was mounted. Neither of the three young horses responded with alarm. Again, the buckskin was the most relaxed. Sullie felt Brady would have been able to take off across the pasture with no trouble. But that would wait.

* * *

Brady stirred under the tree again, then rose, grabbed the Winchester, bridled the sorrel, tightened the cinch. The dog was right beside him, ready to head into the late afternoon toward whatever lay ahead. The dog and Brady had both splashed in the muddy water a bit, and the dog's hair was looking cleaner. Splotchy colored; it was hard to tell if the color came from mud or natural pigmentation. He was still a little lame--always would be, probably--but better than earlier.

They rode steadily for hours, and finally Brady's eyes picked up light in the far distance. A small town. So he was on the right track. He'd see for sure by early morning.

They had passed a couple of small homesteads, lit by kerosene lanterns in smoky windows. A dog had barked but didn't approach, and Brady saw cattle scattered across a field.

Only a few lights suggested a small settlement, and Brady pulled up before he got to lights clustered closer together. The weary trio stopped in a small grove of cottonwoods and prepared for a brief rest before sunrise. The cottonwood leaves had a whispery rattle as a light breeze blew through. Brady had only jerked beef for himself and the dog; the sorrel was happy with a thin stand of prairie grass. A little creek gurgled at the edge of the trees, and all three were grateful for the cool water.

Brady settled himself for a rest after unsaddling the sorrel. He hobbled the horse, aware that there may be more movement of humans and animals this close to the little town. The dog settled himself close to Brady, tired but alert. Both were soon resting quietly, and Brady didn't wait for the bad images to come; he started right away on remembering the first time Sullie had ridden with him. He was hesitant about that at first. He had watched her ride out across the pasture alone on her horse--a nice red roan--and saw that she sat her saddle well and that the horse was quick, responsive, and calm. Still, he worried about being out on the prairie with Sullie. She seemed so fragile, although she was tall and agile. Something in him wanted to protect her. He thought of rattlesnakes, little whirlwinds, fast-coming storms, prairie dog holes. But they did ride out together that first time, and it was comfortable and safe. Their ride was fairly short, but they moved slowly through some grazing cattle, circled a big water hole, topped a rise and rested for a few minutes. They saw no other horses, no other riders. Sullie was relaxed and quiet, spoke only about the cattle and the six horses Brady had nearly ready to turn over to Marsh. His days had become longer, as he worked the first three horses through cattle and tried to expose them to possible spooky things. The last three didn't progress as quickly as the first three, but they were good horses, and Marsh would be able to turn them over to his hands with few worries. Brady wondered about the hands: He had not seen the brothers nor any other hands the whole time he had been at the Marsh ranch. That question was solved the next time he and Sullie rode out together.

They headed west, toward the river, farther than they had

ridden before, and as they topped a low range of gumbo hills, Brady saw a whole layout below: Barn, small house, wellhouse, bunkhouse, corrals.

"This is where my brothers stay, and Dad, too, much of the time," Sullie explained. "Duke is married, and he and Cora live in the house. Dan stays in the bunkhouse with the other hands. Mom and I only see them when they're headed for town for supplies...or if they think Mom has been baking." She grinned. "Duke and Dan work hard, and they'll really put the horses you've been working on to good use." She turned her horse, heading back to the main place. "You'll meet them before long. They'll want to talk to you about the horses, I'm sure. "

Brady was already solemn about the end of his time at the Marsh place. There would be no need for him there when the six horses were turned over to the Marsh brothers. He held his time with those horses and with Sullie close to his insides. The horses were good. Sullie was a treasure. He wanted to see more of her...much more. But how to arrange it? He had no idea of how she felt about any more of a connection. But that was soon settled, too.

When they got back to the corral, Sullie dismounted at the fence and walked over to him. She held her hand up to shield her eyes from the sun, and said, almost business-like, "You'll be leaving soon. I'd like to see more of you. Can we arrange that?"

Brady almost lost his breath. A great development! "Well, yeah, sure...I can ride over...or you can come to my place." He reorganized. "I'd like for you to see my dog and...all of it." Reorganized again. "I'll be here a couple more days, probably to the end of the week. We can make plans for whatever you like." The whole thing was incredible. So fine. Like sunrise and rainbows and plum blossoms, all in one. He unsaddled the bay, brushed him down, turned him into the paddock, and went for his sorrel.

"Does your horse have a name?" she asked.

"Yeah, I guess. I just call him the sorrel, but I think his name was maybe Jake. My dad named him. Long time ago."

"Jake is a good name. Sounds strong. Your dad around

here?"

"Nope. Died four years ago. Snake bite and bad infection. Mom didn't last long after that. Couldn't seem to make it after he was gone."

"Oh gosh, I'm sorry." She frowned and blinked, ill at ease at his answer. He turned away and headed for the road. "Maybe I'll see you tomorrow. We'll see about working something out." He tipped his hat and trotted away.

The next day, old Marsh approached the corral early. "Well, I guess these critters are ready to turn loose to my boys. You've done a fine job. They look good, and I appreciate your help. "

"Thank you, sir. They're a good lot, and I think they're ready to go. I'll be glad to help you any time you have more to break."

"That's good. I'll settle up with you on Friday, and then it'll be a while before we have more to start."

Brady moved to saddle one of the bays, then stopped and faced old Marsh again. "Say, I wonder if you'd like to sell that buckskin. I sure like him."

Marsh answered quickly. "Nah. Sullie wants to keep him for herself. Her brothers aren't gonna like that, since it'll leave them a horse short. But that little roan Sullie rides is gettin' a little age on him, and she needs to have something she can count on."

Brady swallowed disappointment. He had become attached to the buckskin--the smartest of the bunch, so easy going, so quick. "That's too bad. If she changes her mind, let me know. He's a good horse and I can give him a good home."

Strange how things work out. The buckskin did stay with Sullie, but he also went to Brady. There was a brief, real, quiet courtship, and Brady soon found Sullie agreeable to marriage. It wasn't easy for her with her folks, especially her father, but eventually Sullie and the buckskin moved down the road, and Brady had his world in perfect order. The dog...Oscar (Sullie inquired about his name right off)...thought Sullie was just about the best possibility for a housemate, and she fit into the small house as if it were made for her. Brady felt he was the protector for all of them--quiet and strong, like the sorrel. He had a little money, he had good health; he'd make a good life for them.

Chapter 3

Brady thought back on so many good times. And he liked Sullie's folks. Old Marsh was gruff but obviously partial to both women in his life. Sullie rode over to visit them often while Brady was working cattle or riding fence. And the Marshes came regularly for meals or just visits. Sullie's brothers never came, nor did Brady run into them at the Marsh ranch. He'd met them only once--his last day of working the six horses he'd started. Both men were cool and untalkative. When Brady mentioned that to Sullie later, they agreed that the brothers may be a little possessive of their sister. But Sullie added that Duke was by nature a bit sullen and had a quick temper. He and Cora were stand-offish in general, even with old Marsh and Mrs. Marsh.

There were picnics, snowball fights, swimming, cattle work, fence mending, storm watching, cooking experiments, Oscar baths--all of it a treasure. They worked hard, relaxed totally, trusted, loved, laughed, and planned. Through all of it, Sullie and the buckskin moved as partners. His name was Buck. Sullie laughed when she told Brady. "Sorta like 'the sorrel'." Sullie and Buck were a perfect team. Buck responded to her quiet voice commands, moved easily and quickly at the most subtle touch of her leg or change of her position. He had become an exceptional mount.

The cattle sold well, and Sullie surprised Brady by making arrangements with her father to buy a piece of adjoining land at the river's edge. It was a splendid purchase, and old Marsh didn't hesitate long before making the agreement.

"You'll inherit a big part of this place anyway before long, girl. This way I can see you enjoy it before I kick off." His voice was gruff, but he held an arm around Sullie's shoulders as he said it. Brady was well aware of the value of the purchase--to have river-edge property was a huge benefit for their own place. Sullie's brothers, however, were not pleased. Duke was especially critical of the deal, and Brady overheard his loud voice as he ranted to his father about "breaking up the place."

"You don't know what kinda guy Sullie has taken up

with. He might not be around long, and you don't know what he might do with the land. You should cancel this deal right now." Duke sputtered and paced.

But old Marsh remained firm. The land would go to Sullie and Brady with his blessing, and they would share in the final dispersal of the Marsh ranch. He trusted Brady and felt Sullie was safe with him. Also, he admired Brady's care of his own land and buildings and obviously his ability with the horses. It was a good match, and old Marsh felt it would be a lasting one. Mrs. Marsh agreed.

Brady had asked Sullie about Mrs. Marsh's lameness.

"It was a horse accident. Couldn't get her to a good doctor for a while. She didn't heal well. Long time ago." And that's all that was said about it then.

* * *

At sunrise, Brady and his pals readied for the short ride into town. Again, it was jerked beef and water. But Brady promised himself that they would have the benefit of a decent meal--all three of them--in town.

A weather-beaten sign proclaimed the town was Mount Alta. But Brady didn't see much evidence of any "mount"--just a few gentle hills surrounding the houses and stores. They rode into the settlement, Oscar now trotting at point, the sorrel at a fast walk with ears pricked. Brady soon spotted a post office and general store, then a sheriff's office. He rode up to the sheriff's office, dismounted, and approached the door. A small sign named Dalton Hammond as the sheriff, and he was standing just inside the door as Brady entered.

"Hello, stranger. You've got an early start. Welcome to Mount Alta." He stepped forward and offered a hand.

"Thanks, Sheriff. We've ridden quite a ways. Hopin' you can help me locate somebody."

"Sure will try. Who you lookin' for?"

Brady had to pause just a few seconds before he answered calmly. "Man from over east. Name of Duke Marsh." The name put a sour taste in his mouth, a tightening in his gut.

It seemed Hammond hesitated before answering. His voice was firm and quiet. "I gotta ask why you're lookin' for this fella. He in trouble of some kind?"

And Brady couldn't tell the whole story just then but didn't want to misrepresent any of the facts. "He's family-- brother of my wife's. Need to settle some things with him."

The sheriff moved to his desk, picked up a stack of papers and tapped them on the desk top to straighten them. His hands were rough-looking and brown. He didn't seem nervous, just reluctant to answer. "Well, I do know of Duke Marsh. And his wife. They were around here for a couple of weeks but I think they moved on." Hammond seemed to be in his mid-forties, a sturdy man, probably six feet tall. Hair sorta longish and pulled behind his ears. A Bull Durham tag hung from his shirt pocket.

"Moved on to where? What direction? How long ago?" Brady felt sudden impatience. He was on the right track--but now he needed to close the gap.

"Don't rightly know. Left pretty quickly, don't know if they told anybody where they were headed. Might check over at the livery. Mighta got horses from there. Afraid I can't tell you anything else." The sheriff moved back from his desk in a gesture of dismissal.

"Thank you, sir." Disappointment probably colored his words, but at least he was making progress. "I'll head for the livery. Good day, sir." Brady nodded and stepped back through the door. Oscar and the sorrel were waiting, just as they should be, and probably eager to get that decent meal he had in his mind. The livery first, then chow.

The livery was large, close to twenty stalls, clean hay piled inside both the front entry and the rear double doors. Nearly all the stalls were full; several horses stood with their heads over the stall doors.

Brady's eyes adjusted to the dim light inside. At first he saw no one, but soon he caught sight of a skinny guy in a red plaid shirt, greasy hat set back on his head, a bush of curly red hair barely captured.

"Hep ya?" The voice was low and raspy.

"Just need some information."

"Glad to oblige. Here to serve, like they say." The man dusted his palms on the rear of his overalls, then extended a hand.

"Thanks. I'm looking for a man who the sheriff says might have got horses from you recently. Guy by the name of Duke Marsh."

A lifted lip on the man revealed brown teeth, crooked and slightly protruding. "Eeyah. I reckeck him. Don't usually remember names too good, but him and his wife paid big for two good horses from me."

"He say where they were headed?"

"Now I gotta ask why you're after him." His question was the same as the sheriff's: "He in some kinda trouble?"

"Nah. Just family business."

"Well, they headed outa here toward the west. Had bedrolls and a pack mule with 'em. Not too friendly of a fella, if you ask me. Which you didn't."

"Thanks. And do you have a stall for my sorrel? We won't be staying, but he needs a good meal."

The man grinned and moved toward a clean stall near the rear of the livery. "I got a good one right here. Plenty of oats and hay. Water bucket hanging just inside the gate."

Brady moved back out to bring the sorrel in.

"You have help here? The sorrel needs a good rubdown."

"Eeyah. Got a kid comes in around noon every day. He'll do a good job."

Brady unsaddled the sorrel and led him into the stall.

"Good lookin' horse. You get him around here?"

"Nah. Came a good piece. Way east. Okay if I leave my dog here with him while I go fetch us somethin' to eat?"

"Sure. The diner is good. Just up the street." Brady whistled for the dog, motioned him into the stall and told him to stay.

"Back in a minute with dinner, buddy. Just wait here for me."

A bit stiff-legged, Brady walked up the street to a glass-fronted business with a crooked sign announcing "Eats." Inside, a middle-aged woman smiled and pointed to a slate with the day's offerings.

"I'll have the roast beef with gravy and biscuits." The rich smell of beef and fried chicken had stirred the ready appetite in Brady.

"Ya need some green on the plate," said the woman.

"Whaddya got?"

"Beans."

"That'll do. And I'll be needin' another round to take with me. Without the beans."

"Ya got somethin' to carry it in?"

"Nope. Maybe you got an old pie plate or something...?"

"Prob'ly. I'll check."

The meal was served up quickly, and Brady savored every steaming bite. The biscuits were buttery and flaky, the gravy rich, dark brown. He briefly considered apple pie but opted to indulge Oscar instead. The woman came from the back with a pie plate full of meat, potatoes and gravy, and said, "I'm guessin' this is for your critter. I've throwed in a couple of extra biscuits for him. End of the batch, so it's a good use for 'em."

"Thanks a heap. I'll return the pie plate a bit later."

Brady hurried back to the livery, went through the open door. Inside, he saw silhouettes at the far end--a slouched human and what sure looked like Oscar sitting along side. "Who is that with my dog?" he asked the redhead bruskly.

"Name of Harvey Two Shirts. Shows up here occasionally."

"Thanks. I didn't ask your name earlier...?"

"Thompson," said the man. "The Indian won't do no harm to your dog."

Brady walked quickly to the far end of the stable. Oscar sniffed the air, wagged his tail enthusiastically, and moved toward Brady. Brady opened the stall door, started to put the plate down for Oscar when a quick brown hand snatched a biscuit from the top of the plate. Oscar lit into his lunch without delay, and Brady focused on the Indian.

"Why'd you let my dog out?"

"He need air. Not want to shit inside."

"Well, thanks, then."

The Indian brushed crumbs from his mouth, then asked, "Where you go?"

"Lookin' for a man. Guess I'm headed west."

"What man you look for?"

"Name of Duke Marsh. Know him?"

"Seen him."

"I need to get up with him."

"He head for mining camp. Long way. Rough trail."

Brady was astounded. "How do you know this?"

"Heard him say. He think dumb Indian not know English."

Brady paced a few stalls back toward the entrance, turned around, then stopped back at the stall the sorrel was in. Oscar had nearly licked his plate clean and looked like he was almost smiling.

"Say, Harvey. I know your name from Thompson." The Indian looked at him full on. "I'm wondering if you would look after my dog while I'm on the trail of a guy. Depends on the trail and what happens when I catch up with this guy. Might be a week or two."

"Dog is smart. I will look after him for you. No problem." The Indian looked at Brady, at Oscar, at the sorrel. "When we leave?"

"No, you don't understand. I go. YOU stay here with Oscar."

"You want me take care of dog. I take care here. I take care on trail. It is one. Same."

"No. You say it's a rough trail. Oscar is a little lame. It's too much for him."

"Dog can go. If he tired, he ride with me." It was said firmly, positively.

"You maybe didn't understand me. Oscar is old, he's lame. It's too much for him."

"Dog can go. If he tired, he ride with me." Said in the

same manner, no change at all.

"Well, I gotta get a pack mule and some supplies. We'll talk more later."

"No pack mule. Too slow. Catch man with horses only. I bring deer hide for pack on horse."

Brady was frustrated. How did this guy get in control? The Indian was slouchy, dressed in dusty leather. Had hair hanging down to his shoulders, bushy at the ends. An ill-shaped hat shaded his dark face. He didn't weigh much, and he hadn't moved, so Brady had no idea if he was crippled in any way. Hard to tell how old he was.

"You got a horse?" Brady didn't want to encourage the Indian, but he had to get back in charge.

"Got good old horse."

"You bring him by here while I go get supplies, and we'll talk about it some more."

"No talk. I get supplies. You pay." The Indian moved away from the wall, stepped into the aisle of the livery. "We go now." And led the way toward the front entrance. Thompson was nowhere in sight.

Brady and Harvey Two Shirts walked to the general store, stepped inside. Harvey went immediately toward the back of the store and began selecting small packs of merchandise: Candles, matches, salt, coffee, sugar, lard, flour, and meal. Brady added a canteen, then jerked beef, which drew a frown from the Indian. Brady also added a bar of soap, which drew another frown.

"You have plenty money?" asked the Indian.

"Enough for this."

"No need food for dog or horse. Find plenty on trail. Deer, rabbit, birds, snake."

Brady felt more and more as if he were the follower rather than the leader. He paid for their goods and headed back to the livery. Harvey parted ways just ahead of the double doors and gave a brief wave. Brady went inside to his saddle bags, put as much of their purchase as he could into the worn leather. The young boy Thompson had mentioned was in the stall with the sorrel, working quickly and smoothly. The sorrel was looking good, and Oscar was on guard.

"Oscar, I don't know what the hell we're gettin' into," Brady muttered. The kid finished working on the sorrel and Brady handed him a coin. "Thanks. I know he feels good with all that trail dust off him."

"Yes sir. Thank you, sir." And the kid was gone. Brady sat on the ground, his back against the wall, in much the same position as Harvey had been a short while earlier. He tipped his hat forward and dropped his chin. He was almost asleep when he became aware of movement. A shadow, then figures. Harvey was back with his horse.

And what a horse it was. Flea-bitten, washed out, bony, knock-kneed, cow-hocked. Scraggly mane, chopped off tail. Loose lips. Looked ancient.

"Harvey, what are you thinking?! This horse can't make it on any trail, much less a rough one!"

"This old horse good horse. Go better than yours. Go better than any white man horse."

Fatigue settled in on Brady. Harvey Two Shirts was a burden he didn't reckon on, a puzzle he didn't quite know how to handle. He'd made good progress in his quest to catch up to Duke, and he felt he was much closer than he ever had been. The Indian had given him good information...but it was just too chancy to drag him along. And that horse..! It would slow them down, probably cause who knows what kind of trouble...

Harvey had spread a deerskin on the ground and was packing in supplies. He eventually rolled it up and tied it on the back of his...saddle? The piece of equipment was a pad with leather loops hanging down on each side in the place of stirrups. It was leather of some kind, smooth and shiny in parts, deeply scarred in others. There was a thick wad of wool or cotton under it, and it looked to fit the sway back of the old horse to perfection.

"That horse of yours have a name?" asked Brady as a way of stalling the packing procedure.

"Old Horse."

"Yeah. He have a name?"

"Old Horse."

"Yeah. What's his name?"

"Name Old Horse."

"Oh, his name is Old Horse?"

"Yeah. Old Horse. What name are you?"

"Name's Brady Quillan. Sorry I didn't say so before."

"Hmph. I tell you name one day."

The fatigue settled in deeper.

Harvey adjusted his pack a bit, then picked up a shotgun that looked in as bad a shape as his horse. He slipped up on his horse in a quick movement, held his shotgun upright, and nodded at Brady. "We go now."

Brady hesitated just a moment, then quickly bridled and saddled his sorrel, threw the saddle bags into place, mounted, and nodded to Harvey. "I didn't quite know the schedule. We go now."

They moved out of the livery at a walk, turned west, and trotted out of town, Oscar as rearguard. Duke Marsh and his wife were ahead, at the end of a rough trail. And Brady's head was full of determination, memories, revenge, and worry. Harvey Two Shirts was along as guide, resident instructor, caretaker, mystic, and who knows what else.

Chapter 4

For the first hour, Brady kept a close eye on Harvey Two Shirts, watching how his horse moved, how Harvey chose which branches of the trail to follow. Harvey and his horse made a conspicuous shape: Pouches and rolls poked out at various angles; the Indian slouched, the horse wobbled occasionally. Remarkably, the packs made no sound, even though they contained cooking pots and various tools. Apparently Harvey had packed them with enough food and soft gear to muffle any possible sound.

Occasionally Brady heard a mumbling, sighing voice from Harvey, but it wasn't a song and it wasn't conversation. Harvey rode with his feet swinging free from the loops on his "saddle"; his reins often hung loose on Old Horse's withers. His gun was moved from upright, balanced on his thigh, to loosely slung under his arm. It was a puzzle to Brady at first that Old Horse moved in a sort of single-foot--and was as fast at that gait as the sorrel was at an easy lope. Harvey Two Shirts sat his horse completely at ease, relaxed and fluid.

Brady figured they were making good time--but it was hard to figure, since he had only a vague idea of how far the mining camp might be. They alternated their speed, kept watch for small creeks and ponds to water their horses and fill their canteens. There was no conversation. Brady settled his mind about Harvey -- temporarily, anyway--and let his memories come back.

* * *

The trouble with Duke and Cora didn't accelerate until the day Brady found Cora on the piece of land Sullie had bought from old Marsh. Cora halted her horse when she caught sight of Brady.

Brady spoke first. "Good morning. How'd you happen to get over here?"

Cora pursed her lips, jerked her horse around to face him, then almost snarled. "This land rightfully belongs to Duke and me, not to you. I'm lookin' it over to be sure nothing has been done to decrease its value."

Brady was startled. Although he knew Duke and Cora were against the deal, he had no idea there were lingering resentments. "We take good care of all our land, and you can see, just like you, we've been lucky with the rain."

"This land should be ours. And it WILL be ours," she sputtered, then kicked her horse into a gallop and headed back toward Marsh land.

Brady was concerned and irked. Duke had always been standoffish, and Cora, too. He knew the deed was solid, that old Marsh was satisfied with the deal they had made. He knew also that Duke was short-tempered, might hold a grudge, and that trouble may be ahead. He headed back to the house to talk with Sullie about it.

"He's my brother, but we haven't ever been close, " she said. "I was young when it happened, but he was involved in my mother's accident, and I've never forgiven him for that."

Brady remembered that Sullie had told him her mom's lameness came from a horse accident, but there hadn't been any details.

"Mom was riding a young horse, and Duke was practicing his roping. He threw a loop over Mom's horse, spooked him, and the horse ran and fell, trapping Mom beneath him." Sullie brushed hair out of her face, then continued. "Maybe I should have been more understanding...but Duke had been warned before about being careful around the young horses. He made a bad mistake. And he didn't seem to be sorry for it. It was more like he was trying to blame Mom, saying she should have had better control over her horse."

Brady moved to put his arm around Sullie.

"We couldn't get Mom to help for two days, and then the wagon ride was rough on her. The doctor did the best he could, but there were broken bones that didn't set right. It was a long, hard healing process for her. She doesn't complain, but I know she still has a lot of pain sometimes."

"We can look after her whenever she needs it. And we

can look after our own place, too--which means we need to keep an eye on Duke and Cora. What do you think they have in mind?"

"I don't know. One thing I DO know: They are both strong, determined people....and greedy. They'll do whatever needs to be done to get what they want."

Things went smoothly for a while, but Brady and Sullie both kept an eye out for anything the least bit out of order: A fence wire broken, a small fire burning in a ditch, cattle moved far beyond where they normally grazed, two horses sweated up as if they had been running, a calf on the wrong side of the fence, separated from its mother. Little things that could have just been coincidence or bad luck, but considering the situation....

Old Marsh had not mentioned anything to Brady about working more horses. Brady wondered if that might be because Duke had campaigned against it or maybe just because Old Marsh was cutting down a bit. Marsh was not really old, but Brady had noticed he had slowed down. On a cool spring morning, Brady was surprised to see Marsh riding up to the front gate.

"Hello, sir. Glad to see you out this morning. Everything okay?"

The older man halted his horse, then sat with his hands crossed on the saddle horn. "Yeah, mostly okay. Got a little problem I need to talk to you about."

"Come on in. There's still coffee on the stove."

The men moved into the small kitchen. Sullie greeted her father with a hug and got mugs and a plate of buns for the two men. Old Marsh sweetened and lightened his coffee, then took a small sip.

"I gotta tell you, I'm not feelin' as good as I should these days." He looked straight at Brady, then continued. "I think maybe something's a little off--heart, maybe. I've had a little pain, get tired awful quick, don't sleep too good." His gray eyes stayed focused on Brady. "I've got a concern about the boys, Brady. There's something goin' on, and I don't quite know what it is. Duke and Cora are pressuring me to change my will, and

Dan seems to be goin' along with 'em."

Brady and Sullie both stiffened, and Brady felt a tightening in his gut. He cared a great deal for Marsh, and it was painful to hear the older man's concerns. Marsh continued, "I'm not makin' any changes. I've got things worked out the way I want, but it's worrisome to have those boys and Cora at me so much."

"Do you need to go in to the doc? We can take you in the wagon any time you want to go."

"Nah, not yet. I just wanna talk to you about being real careful to notice anything a little off on your place. I'm thinking there may be sabotage of some kind in the minds of these guys. Mebbe tryin' to spook you a little."

"We've noticed a couple of things, but Marsh, we're not goin' anywhere, if that's their plan. This is our home, they are family, like it or not, and we're not fixin' to get involved in anything rough."

Sullie looked at him with affection, and he knew he had spoken for both of them.

"That's what I hoped. But you gotta be careful. Duke is rash, and that Cora can be downright mean. I've seen her handle some people in town in a real bad way."

"We'll look out. And we'll be lookin' out for you, too." He sipped his coffee. "Miz Marsh okay? She worried about this situation, too?"

"She keeps it to herself. But she's tough; she'll make it through whatever happens."

Old Marsh stood, put out his hand to Brady. "Son, you're a fine man for Sullie, and I like how the two of you have handled things." He put an arm around his daughter, then stepped to the door. Brady and Sullie watched as he got on his horse and rode away. They were still for a few moments, then moved quietly to the corral and barn to get started on the day's work. Buck walked quickly up to Sullie when she came into the corral, then followed her as she scooped manure. Brady noticed Buck's feed pan held a little more grain than the pans of the other horses, and Sullie often stood by him as he ate, rubbing him and talking to him quietly. The bond between them was mutual, that was obvious.

* * *

The sun was lowering, and Brady felt they should be looking to the distance for a camp site. Harvey was ahead of him, though, and was already looking toward gray hills a few miles away. Hard to tell from this far, but there might be trees and a creek ahead.

The sky was dark when they came to a small stand of trees. There was a creek, and plenty of dead wood on the ground for a small fire. They unsaddled their horses, hobbled them, then started clearing a small place for the fire. Harvey disappeared as Brady moved stones to form a pit. He found a pan and the coffee pot, got water and looked for the coffee grounds. He had just started a small fire when Harvey returned, swinging a small cottontail from his hand.

"I didn't hear a shot. How'd you get that?"

"Slingshot. Not cost like shells," Harvey grunted, then squatted and started skinning the rabbit. In no time at all, the rabbit was sizzling and dripping over the fire, and Harvey was mixing up some kind of concoction in the pan. He reached into the pack and pulled out the pie pan from the restaurant in Mount Alta.

"Oh damn," muttered Brady. "I was supposed to take that back."

"Lady there is good lady. We take it back when we go."

Harvey scooped out some of the doughy mixture, then pulled off a small strip of the hot meat and put it down before Oscar with a hand out before him to caution the dog. Oscar had good manners, sniffed the meal, then carefully nibbled the dough.

"I take care of dog," grunted the Indian.

"Looks like you're taking care of all of us," acknowledged Brady. "Smells good. Whaddya call this stuff in the pan?"

"Wajapi. Frybread. Fill belly." Harvey scooped out a chunk and handed it to Brady. It tasted fine. Bland but fine.

With the rabbit, it was a feast after a long afternoon in the saddle.

The horses had prairie grass and plenty of water. Oscar, like Brady, was tired but full. Brady had no idea if Harvey Two Shirts might be tired but he was pretty sure he was full. Rabbit skin and innards were buried. Bedrolls were smoothed out, the cooking fire doused, and both men stretched out. Again, there was no conversation.

As Brady relaxed into a light sleep, he thought again back to the tension among the Marshes he and Sullie felt was rapidly increasing.

Chapter 5

Brady was working on a rail for the front porch of the house when a rider approached. He recognized the horse as one of Marsh's but didn't know the rider.

"Howdy. Can I help you?" he called from the porch.

"Yeah. I come from Duke Marsh. We're short of horseflesh. He needs that buckskin there in the corral."

"Sorry, can't oblige. I can help you find another one that'll work for you."

"Duke wants the buckskin, nothing else."

"Like I say, he's not available. Come on over to the corral and see if there's something else for you."

"Duke's not gonna like this. I was told to bring the buckskin, not nothin' else."

"Sorry to disappoint you, but that's the way it is."

The rider jerked his horse around and headed back toward the Marsh place at a gallop. Brady exhaled, pushed his hat back on his head, then stepped through the front door. "Sullie? You hear that guy?"

Sullie stepped quickly toward Brady, a look of concern and disgust on her face. "Yes. That's Dutch Heisler. He's one of Duke's hired hands. But I don't get this demand. Why would Duke insist on borrowing Buck?"

"Dunno. Maybe because he's seen how good Buck is. Maybe because he knows Buck is special to you. Maybe...who knows?"

"We have to be real careful. Let's keep Buck in the barn when we're not right out here close to the corral. I don't think anybody could grab him with Oscar here on watch, but folks are sneaky, and you never know."

Several days went by with no more sign of Duke's hired man. Then on a day Brady and Sullie had taken the wagon into town for supplies, they came back to find the barn door open, Oscar lying, unmoving, in front of the house. Brady went immediately to Oscar; Sullie went to check the barn.

Oscar was breathing; Buck was gone.

It was a devastating blow to both of them. Both were devoted to Oscar and Buck, both felt inept to deal with either emergency. Brady carried Oscar to the porch, got cool water to pat him down, felt his skull and the rest of the body for bumps or broken bones. There was only a big lump on his head and another on his left shoulder blade. An abrasion on his left shoulder, but no blood, no bones sticking through skin.

Sullie was checking for hoofprints along the fence and the road in. She came back to the porch to report that it looked as if only one rider had led Buck out. Her eyes were tear-filled but her jaw was firm. "I'm going over to see Dad about this. He'll know how to handle it."

"Be real careful. I'll stay here to look after Oscar, see if I can get him to come to."

Sullie was gone for only a couple of hours. Old Marsh had tried to calm her, told her he hadn't known of Duke's plan to take Buck, assured her he'd get Buck back to her right away. In the meantime, Brady had watched Oscar carefully, finally determining there might be a chip broken off the shoulder bone on the left.

Oscar whined, tried to lift his head. Brady calmed him, speaking quietly and patting his back. It was a huge relief to see him conscious, but Brady figured it would be a long healing process. Oscar was a lively dog, and pain would limit his activities, for sure. Brady didn't know how to relieve Oscar's pain...or Sullie's.

Three more days went by. No sign of Buck. But Oscar was able to limp around a bit, and he was eating. Sullie went about her chores with a constant eye toward her family's ranch.

On the fourth day, Mrs. Marsh drove up in a buckboard. Both Brady and Sullie rushed to meet her. Something was obviously bad wrong for her to come alone, and there was worry on her face.

"What is it, Mom?" Sullie moved to put a hand on her mother's arm.

"It's your dad. He's had a heart attack, I think. He's been in awful pain, out of his head, can't even talk at all sometimes."

Brady responded quickly. "We'll go back with you. Maybe we can get him to town for help."

Sullie climbed into the buckboard beside her mother, and Brady went to saddle a horse. It took little time to get to the Marsh place, and Sullie and her mother went into the house immediately. Brady pulled up shortly after, and he, too, went inside. Old Marsh was in bed--gray, rasping in shallow breaths, not moving. The big man looked shrunken.

"I don't think we oughta move him, " Brady said in a low voice. "Let me ride into town and see if I can get the doc to come out here."

Sullie and her mother agreed.

"Where are Duke and Dan?" asked Sullie.

"Over at the other place. They know he's not well. They had argued about that buckskin, and Duke took off in a hurry. Your father had told Duke to take that horse back to you right away, and he didn't like that one bit."

"We'll settle that when Marsh is better. I'll head into town right now."

But it was too late when Brady returned with the doctor. Old Marsh hadn't lasted even the short while it took for Brady to make the trip with the doctor in hand. Both Sullie and her mother were stoic but obviously in deep grief. Neither of the boys was there.

"Should I ride over to the other place to get Duke and Dan?" asked Brady.

Mrs. Marsh answered quietly. "I don't think that's a good idea. There's bad feelings with those boys, and Cora doesn't help it one bit. Let me and Sullie and the doctor take care of Marsh, get him ready for ... well, you just let me handle the boys and Cora."

"Brady, I'll stay here with Mom, and you go back to our place. I'll come when I can."

The next few days were bleak but busy. Old Marsh was buried at his ranch. Only a few friends were there, and the burial was brief. It was Brady, not Duke or Dan, who filled the grave. It was Sullie who helped the small group of mourners to a meal at the ranch house. Cora had put in only a brief appearance, her pinched face cold and unwelcoming to visitors; then she was no longer in sight. And, Sullie noticed, neither was Buck. He had to be over at the other place, and she would make it a point to find him.

Mrs. Marsh was solemn but strong, dealing with the few friends who came by in the days after the burial. Sullie had told Brady her mother had always been totally involved in the running of the ranch, that the finances and handling of the livestock would be carried on as if old Marsh were still in charge. Sullie felt there would be problems, that Duke would want to take over completely rather than just handle things at the smaller place.

A week after the burial, Sullie headed back over to her family's ranch, determined to find Buck and bring him home. She stopped by the main house to speak first to her mother, then rode on to Duke's headquarters. No one seemed to be at the house or in the barnyard. She rode toward the corral, dismounted at the corral fence, and looped her reins over a post. There were two horses in the corral, both in the shade of barn and hard to see at first. She moved closer, saw that both horses were in bad shape--heads down, hunched over. She moved closer still and her heart stopped. One of the horses was Buck--nearly unrecognizable, his coat matted and dirty, his mane and tail tangled. But worse than that, he was terribly thin, gaunt, his ribs sticking out. She called to him. At first he didn't respond. Then, slowly, slowly, he lifted his head and looked toward her. His ears pricked forward, one at a time, and then he moved. But God, he was lame! He could hardly move, dragged his feet and bobbed his head close to the ground. But he moved toward her, slowly but surely. Fighting back tears, Sullie climbed the board fence and met him in the center of the corral. She could hardly believe this was Buck--how could this have happened in such a short while? And how was she going to be able to get him home when he could hardly move at all?

Buck put his nose against her leg and flapped his lips a couple of times. Sullie could hardly keep from crying out loud.

She moved her hands over him, feeling for swelling or cuts, smoothed his tangled mane with her fingers as best she could. She was startled when a voice spoke behind her.

"Whaddya doin' here?" It was Duke, astride a horse at the corral fence.

"What has happened to this horse?!? What have you done? Why do you even have him?"

"Well, we needed him. I put Dutch on him for a few days to work the kinks outa him. Seems he doesn't have much stayin' power." Duke's tone was sarcastic, his face a sour mask of haughty power.

"You're crazy, and you've nearly killed him! Dad told you to bring him back to me, and now he's hardly able to move." Sullie knew she was yelling, knew she was having little effect on Duke, but she was powerless in her fury. "And Oscar! What in the hell did you do to our dog? He's nearly dead, too!" Sweat and tears mixed on her cheeks as she glared at the brother she felt she could no longer trust, no longer deal with at all, no longer even claim as kindred.

Duke sneered again. "Dutch had a little problem with him. Said he had to tune him up a bit."

"You are a criminal, you know. What you've done is illegal! And I'll contact the sheriff, and you'll answer for it." She headed for the corral fence, relieved that Duke was not real close to her horse.

"Well, Cora has already been in touch with the sheriff, matter of fact." Duke adjusted his hat, then continued. "We'll be talking to the judge soon to get the property thing settled. Dad didn't know what he was doing when he wrote those last things for that lawyer fella."

Sullie had no idea what he was talking about, just knew that she needed to get to Brady for help with Buck, needed to escape the mean presence of her brother.

"I'll be back to get Buck. And if you have any sense at all, you won't be around. And he better be in better shape than he is right now when I come back." She mounted her horse and left, eager to put distance between them. Duke looked after her, smiling a grim smile. Cora would be interested to hear of this development.

Chapter 6

Brady awoke suddenly, startled to find Harvey Two Shirts leaning over him, holding his shoulder firmly.

"You make noise. Too loud. Oscar try to sleep," grunted the Indian.

"Oof. Musta had a bad dream." Brady rose to a sitting position, rubbing his forehead and neck.

"No dream. Day worry, night worry, both one. Same."

"I tell ya, it was a dream. Happens sometimes."

"Day worry, night worry, both one. Same. What you worry?"

"Harvey, don't go where you don't have business. It's not a thing for you to think about." Brady looked toward the east, trying to figure how close sunrise might be. Quite a spell off, it seemed.

"I think Duke Marsh is you worry. Why we follow him?" Harvey wasn't going to give it up.

Brady gave a drawn-out sigh, then sat up straighter. He started telling Harvey the long tale of Duke, Dan, Old Marsh... and Sullie. He tried to tell it straight, as briefly as possible, but as honestly as he could. Harvey periodically grunted or stared more intensely at Brady. Brady had gotten as far in his telling as Sullie's finding Buck in terrible shape when Harvey stood and moved toward the packs. "Time to eat," he grunted. Brady squinted toward the east again; still didn't see any sign of sunrise.

"We start early, make good time. Duke Marsh need eyopehyah. Punish. Man bad to horse do bad to all things. Need punish."

Brady agreed, appreciating the Indian's immediate discernment of the character of Duke Marsh. Not to mention Cora or Dutch Heisler.

Coffee and frybread made the meal, and it took little time to saddle and pack the horses. Oscar gobbled up his frybread and had a good slug of creek water before they headed for the dim trail. There was finally at least a slight suggestion of a lighter shade of dark as they headed out.

When daylight finally came, the prairie stretched out forever ahead of them. The horses had energy and Oscar trotted along without much of a limp. A cool breeze blew from behind them, and the prairie grass moved in waves. Harvey asked no questions, made no comments, merely continued his tuneless humming.

They rode steadily for several hours, pausing only at one small creek to water the critters and themselves. Brady offered Harvey a piece of jerked beef, which Harvey accepted with a scowl. Oscar also accepted a piece, and they moved on.

Midafternoon, Harvey Two Shirts slowed and motioned for Brady to come up along side him.

"Where you wife now?" Harvey asked abruptly.

"She's dead," Brady said quietly.

"How she die?"

"Shot."

"Who shoot?"

"I thought Duke or Cora. Maybe even Duke's hired hand, Dutch Heisler."

"You not know in you head which one?"

"No. Not at first. I didn't see. Whoever it was shot from the corner of a building, then stepped back out of sight, took off on horseback, and I couldn't move fast enough to see."

"Why they shoot?"

Brady tried to organize his thoughts in his head, tried to line up events so they would make sense to Harvey Two Shirts. He started by explaining how Sullie had ridden back and forth to the Marsh ranch daily to treat Buck, how she finally got him strong enough to walk the five miles back to their place. How Oscar had made progress, healing slowly until he could get around pretty well again. How Sullie had helped her mother as much as she could, how she rode over nearly every day to check on her. She learned from Mrs. Marsh that her father had been dealing with some lawyer fella and had made some changes to his plans. Duke, Cora, and Dan were upset about it, but Sullie didn't know the details and was too concerned with helping her mother and looking after her own critters to worry about it.

Weeks went by with little contact between Sullie and her brothers and Cora. Mrs. Marsh had mentioned that Cora had been very difficult to deal with, that there was constant criticism of the way Mrs. Marsh handled the ranch business. Sullie had arrived at the ranch one morning to find Cora in the kitchen of the big house, one hand on her hip, the other pointing a finger at Mrs. Marsh's face.

"You have no right to do what you did!" Cora shouted.

Mrs. Marsh was calm but obviously disgusted with the young woman. "Just go back to the other place and settle down."

"Settle down?!? How can I settle down when you've taken a huge chunk of our assets? And who knows what you'll be doing with it!" Cora seemed to notice just then that Sullie was standing behind her. "And YOU!! What the hell are YOU doing here?! Haven't you done enough already?"

Sullie was lost in the conversation, had no idea what she might have done to upset Cora so totally.

"I don't know why you're upset, Cora, but Mom is right. You should just go back home and calm down."

"This IS my home!" Cora yelled. "Every inch of it! It's not yours or your crooked husband's. It's MINE!"

Brady had seen in his mind how it must have been for Sullie to witness, and he replayed it for Harvey. He tried to shorten his recollection of events, make the unpleasant telling brief and clear.

"We didn't know it at the time, but old Marsh had changed his plans so that he would leave Sullie and me the big place, left the other place for Duke and Dan to share. It was a huge blow to the brothers, but Marsh had seen that Cora and Duke were becoming more greedy...and more dishonest."

Brady had to get his thoughts in line again. The telling, speaking of it aloud, was uncomfortable for him, especially since he didn't really know how much Harvey Two Shirts was absorbing.

"The final blow was when Mrs. Marsh added Sullie's name to all the bank accounts and made it impossible for Duke and Cora to tap into any of the Marsh cash."

Harvey had been quiet throughout the telling, and his only response had been a squinting of his eyes or a slow movement of his head from side to side.

* * *

The terms of Marsh's legal decision weren't instituted immediately. Mrs. Marsh was to maintain control until she was sixty or sixty-five years old, then she would move in with Sullie and Brady, if that was agreeable to them. The arrangement was, of course, just fine with them, and all three would have enjoyed the close company....if it had worked out that way.

A January blizzard made Sullie's visits to the big place impossible for a few days. When she was finally able to make the ride, she found her mother gravely ill, lying on the sofa with blankets wrapped around her, the house cold, no fire in the stove, no wood inside available to burn. Sullie hurried to care for her, carried wood from the wood pile, got the stove putting out heat, fixed her mother tea and soup. There was nothing in the way of medicine for her mother. She cleaned her as best as she could and worried that Brady would be expecting her back at their place. She could not leave her mother; she couldn't move her.

Sullie put her horse in the barn, carried more wood in, and settled herself for the evening. Brady would figure something was wrong and would eventually come to check. Mrs. Marsh needed to be kept warm and fed. No one was there to do that except Sullie. No sign whatsoever of Duke, Cora, or Dan.

Brady did come the next day, having made the trip through deep snow and high wind. Mrs. Marsh had made no improvement, and Sullie and Brady were faced with the same predicament they had when old Marsh had his heart attack. Except this time it was worse: It was unlikely the doctor would agree to even try to make the trip from town to the ranch. Maybe he would send medicine with Brady; that would be their only hope. Brady saddled one of the Marsh horses and left for town--a long, cold ride.

Mrs. Marsh did rouse herself midmorning and after coughing and struggling for breath, indicated to Sullie she needed to talk. Her voice was weak and breathy, her words hard to understand.

"Sullie, dear, you must be careful....Duke and Cora...don't trust them....your father...knew how they are...tried to save the ranch for you...he trusted you...and Brady....be strong...guard the land..." The little lady wheezed and then was quiet. Sullie gently patted her arm, adjusted the quilts, wiped her mother's brow.

"Don't worry, Mom. We'll handle it."

Sullie thought back to the day when Duke had taunted that Cora had already contacted the sheriff. That had been a while back, and neither she nor Brady had followed through on their threat to charge Duke with theft and cruelty. It was "outa sight, outa mind", and the less contact they had with Sullie's brothers and Cora, the better. They hadn't been able to think of a reason for Duke to mishandle Buck to such a horrible degree. Dutch Heisler's cruelty to Oscar they figured was his basic rough, evil nature.

In the afternoon, Mrs. Marsh again awakened, took a sip of broth, coughed, and whispered,"Sullie...the combination...for the safe...is your birthday....All you need....is there. You're...a...fine...daughter." Her eyelids fluttered and she breathed out a long, quiet breath and then was silent. Sullie listened for her breathing, tried to feel a pulse, then admitted to herself she was too upset to detect either.

It was dark when Brady returned. He clomped snow off his boots and handed Sullie a small package. "Doc can't come. Weather too bad and he has patients in town in bad shape. How's Miz Marsh?"

He looked then at Sullie, at her pale, grief-stricken face, her slumped shoulders, her trembling hands.

"Oh Christ. Sullie, I'm so sorry, so sorry." His embrace gave her warmth and she leaned into it. She was a strong woman, but this was as hard as the death of her father, and she wondered if she had the reserves to handle it. Thank God for Brady. And Brady thought, "Thank God for Sullie. And her strength."

Chapter 7

Brady and Harvey moved steadily. In the late afternoon, Oscar's lameness had become worse. Harvey dismounted, picked Oscar up smoothly and set him on the "saddle", then vaulted up behind him with no effect at all on Oscar's balance. Harvey settled himself firmly behind the dog, then nudged Old Horse forward. It looked almost as if a child were in front of Harvey, and Oscar looked as if he could ride point from that position as well as from the ground. Harvey was for sure true to his word: He would care for Oscar.

They rode at a quick pace, moving directly west across the prairie. It was nearly dusk when they sighted a small cabin with an outbuilding and small corral. Harvey changed course slightly to avoid the possibility of human contact, and Brady was in agreement. They were nearly out of sight of the little place when Harvey pulled up short.

"Horse come," he grunted. And sure enough, a rider was galloping toward them. Harvey and Brady pulled up, sat waiting for the rider to approach to within talking distance.

It was a middle-aged man, whiskery and burley, his horse lanky.

"We don't get much travelers around here," the man said in an aggressive tone. "Where you headed?"

Brady nodded, then spoke quietly. "Headed west."

"I can see that," the man snarled. "Where to?"

"Just west."

"What's the Injun for? You takin' him in for some thievin' or somethin'?"

"Nah." Brady adjusted his hat and nudged the sorrel to movement. "We'll be headin' on."

"Can't that Injun talk at all?" the man persisted.

"Don't ever have much to say." Which was the truth, Brady thought to himself.

"Why's that dog sittin' up there like that?"

"He's headed west, too, and we'll be headin' on now."

Brady and Harvey both moved their horses away from

the man, eager to put distance betwen them before the man became more hostile.

"Well, just keep on a-goin'. Don't think about restin' anywhere near my land. Not nowhere near. And you got a ways to go before yer offa my land."

Brady didn't respond, just followed Harvey on across the prairie. The man sat his horse, still, watching as they moved off toward the darkening western sky. The man wasn't wearing a gun, didn't have one in a scabbard, but he seemed threatening nevertheless. Brady was eager to put miles between them before settling for the night. Harvey, however, didn't seem concerned. He was already looking for trees and water.

A couple of miles farther, Harvey moved toward a small stand of cottonwoods. "Water here," he announced. "Oscar say time for eat." If Harvey's face ever betrayed a sense of amusement, there might be one now. Not a smile, just a relaxing of his jaw.

They stopped amid the cottonwoods and Brady dismounted and moved to lift Oscar from his perch. On the ground, the dog stretched, yawned, and then wagged his tail, suggesting it WAS time to eat. Harvey was correct again--there was a small pond of water amid the trees, and Brady thought maybe they were pretty close to the river.

They quickly cleared an area for their bedrolls and for a fire pit. Again Harvey disappeared briefly, then came back with two small fish hanging from a leather thong. "Not much fish here. Enough with wajapi." Harvey fried the fish in a bit of lard, and the aroma was enough to make Brady's mouth water. Again, the wajapi was tasty, and all three shared equally in the panful.

The horses were watered at the pond, led to a grassy area, hobbled, and left to graze. Oscar and the men prepared to settle for the night at the base of a couple of trees. Harvey, as always, was quiet. Brady felt compelled to state his unease about the man at the little homestead.

"I don't really trust that guy back there."

"He no good. Might come tonight. Try to steal."

"Why in the world didn't we go farther?" Brady sputtered. "Why make it easy for him?"

"This good place for rest," Harvey grunted. "Also good place for haychaydu. Correct."

"You mean, wait for the guy to come?"

"Yes. Teach lesson. Correct. Haychaydu."

Harvey brushed dirt over their fire. "Keep gun close."

Brady and Oscar settled into their places on the ground; Harvey rested in a sitting position at the base of a cottonwood. All three were totally quiet in a matter of minutes. As always, Brady occupied his mind with memories.

* * *

Brady and Sullie made the trip to town a couple of weeks after Mrs. Marsh's death with the aim of determining just what the property settlement was and the extent of the assets at the bank. Sullie had opened the safe at the ranch and found her father's will, Mrs. Marsh's will, bank books, deeds, and cash. There was a great deal of paperwork, and it all looked in order, but they both felt they needed the insight of a professional.

The lawyer was prepared for them, having heard of the death of Mrs. Marsh, and as they sat in his office, he was forthright in his explanation of their situation.

"Mrs. Marsh was careful, and she was firm in her belief that the two of you would be the best guardians of the Marsh legacy. She would have cut Duke and Dan completely off if she hadn't been concerned about the animosity already existing on the part of those two boys and Duke's wife." He adjusted his glasses, shuffled the papers briefly. "I've heard quite a bit about those boys, and I have to say I agree with her."

The conference went smoothly, and Brady and Sullie left the lawyer's office feeling well informed and well advised as well as fortunate but concerned about the responsibility of running the big holding. Their next stop was the sheriff's office.

Brady explained to the sheriff their concern about Duke's earlier behavior and inquired about any legal action about which the sheriff may have knowledge.

"Well, that woman came in here, wantin' us to do somethin' about changin' fence lines on the Marsh property." The sheriff rubbed his jaw. "I tried to tell her she needed a lawyer or a judge--not us. She didn't wanna listen."

Brady nodded. He and Sullie both knew Cora would try legal means--and any other means--to guarantee what she wanted done.

"Far as I know, they didn't get up with anybody in town. Maybe looked somewhere else for legal help. That's all I know." The sheriff seemed pleasant enough, and Brady figured that was all the information they would get.

"Thanks, sir. We'll be outa your way."

"You bet. Good luck."

It would take good luck, and lots of it, to get things straightened out between Sullie's brothers, Cora, and themselves. Brady and Sullie would keep the ranch records as carefully as they could, tend the livestock and land diligently, and hope for the best.

* * *

Brady felt a soft nudge. Harvey was leaning over him.

"Horse come."

Brady sat up quickly, moved his Winchester to his hand, and listened intently. He heard nothing. But he knew Harvey was likely right, that someone was approaching. Harvey moved silently to another cottonwood. Both men were ready to handle whoever it was that was headed into their campsite.

Finally Brady heard a shuffle of hoofs and the creak of a saddle. Somebody had dismounted. Seconds passed, then minutes. Brady heard the sorrel snort, then move. He looked through the darkness toward Harvey. Harvey motioned to move toward the horses, and both men stepped silently in that direction. Brady saw a large figure loop a rope over the sorrel's head, then stoop to loosen the hobbles.

"Hold it!" Brady's voice shot out through the darkness as he cocked the Winchester. Harvey moved quickly to the side of the intruder, a knife in one hand and his old gun in the other.

"Step away from that horse and lift your hands."

The man moved slightly, grumbled, and faced Brady. "I told you to stay off my property," he snarled.

"I'm thinking you don't own this land, and you sure don't have any business around my horse."

"You don't know shit about who owns what." The man's voice was louder now, and he moved closer toward Brady.

"Stay right where you are. Harvey, check him for a pistol."

Harvey approached the man, still holding knife and gun. The man suddenly sprang for Harvey, arms out to crush him in a bear hug. Harvey's knife flashed and the man fell back, a grunt and then a yell coming from him.

"Don't try stupid stuff, fella," Brady warned, then came toward the injured man. "I told you, stay right where you are."

Harvey motioned toward the man's feet. At first Brady didn't understand what Harvey wanted, but then got the idea. "Take your boots off," he ordered the man, backing up his order with a movement of the Winchester.

The man stooped to pull off his boots, one at a time.

"Socks, too," ordered Brady. The man complied.

Harvey picked up the boots and socks, went toward the man's horse, grabbed the gun from the scabbard, walked quickly toward the pond and threw it all in.

"The hell you think you're doin'?" hollered the man.

"You won't be needin' it here," muttered Brady. Harvey went back to the man's horse, removed the bridle, then whacked the horse on the rump, guaranteeing a quick departure. "You won't be needin' that horse, either. You can make it back to your place on foot."

The man growled, then made a desperate move for Brady. He had made it to Brady's shoulder when Harvey stepped in. Harvey bent down, his knife flashing again, and the man fell sideways. "The hell....oh shit!" A loud moan, and then the man yelled again. "You crippled me!"

And Harvey HAD crippled him, slashing the man's Achilles tendon.

"It'll take you a little longer this way, but that was your choice." Brady said it in a firm, dry voice. "Now git on outa here. Back to your own place."

"You can't do this to me," whined the man. "You can't expeck me to make it back like this."

"We had to teach you a lesson. Haychaydu." Brady threw his neck rag down to the man. "Wrap that ankle in this. It'll help."

It wouldn't be long until dawn, so Brady and Harvey readied their horses to travel. They'd eat later on in the morning, when there would be no unpleasant company. They didn't bother to look back to watch the wounded man hobble toward his homestead. It would be a long, painful trip for him, but it was haychaydu.

After a spell of quiet trotting, Brady slowed and asked Harvey a question he'd been harboring for a while. "Why don't you talk when we're around people? You're in charge of this venture as much as I am, and you know all the details. Seems you'd speak up. And you sure could have told that guy back there what to do."

Harvey didn't answer immediately. "Quiet dumb Indian, quiet smart Indian. It is one. Same. White man want to know. Smart or dumb. If I speak, he will know."

Brady didn't quite follow Harvey's thinking on this point. Nevertheless, he would respect Harvey's actions. He had another question. "That was a pretty rough lesson for that guy back there. He'll always be a cripple."

"He make bad move. First haychaydu not enough for him. Need more."

And another question: "Why'd you throw his gun in the pond? You maybe could have used that."

"Got good gun already."

That made sense to Brady, and he had new respect for Harvey's ability to defend himself as well as looking after Brady, Oscar, and the horses. Harvey was much quicker and stronger than he looked. And he had a firm set of standards. Brady had to admit Harvey was a valuable companion. Valuable...and maybe quite a little unpredictable.

Chapter 8

Progress was good. The day was cooler, the horses had good energy, and Oscar's ride the day before had eased his lameness. They had jerked beef for a quick lunch, filled canteens from a cold running creek, and were back on the trail quickly. The sorrel was content to follow Old Horse, and Brady's mind went to developments at the Marsh ranch that led up to the final tragedy that prompted the current venture.

Duke hadn't come around the Marsh house while Brady and Sullie were there, and neither had seen Dan or Cora for nearly a month. Sullie had straightened her mother's belongings, kept the house clean and tidy, but she and Brady didn't consider moving in. It wasn't a long ride between the two places, and they made the trip often. Brady was able to look after the Marsh cattle as well as their own, and Duke's spread was far enough away that the herds didn't mix. He and Sullie had discussed the possibility of selling off some of the Marsh cattle as well as some of their own, consolidating the herds, making it more practical to look after both places. Brady had inquired in town about the availability of a hired hand to live at the Marsh place and generally look after things there, with Brady's help. So far, no one had seemed suitable. They would need to find someone before the next cold season. Snow made the trip between the two places too difficult to do on a daily basis.

There were no bad incidents until the day Dutch approached Sullie as she rode into the Marsh place early one morning. Brady planned to come later in the day, after he finished chores at their own place.

"Hello, little missy. I see you're not ridin' that buckskin yet. Been several weeks now. 'S'amatter? He not tough enough to do it any more?" Dutch's voice was mocking, ugly. He was ugly in general: Big, square face, whiskered and discolored; tobacco-stained teeth and corners of his mouth, dirty hair and clothing.

Sullie didn't answer, just kept heading toward the main gate at the ranch.

"Now don't be havin' bad manners. I need to talk to you about a deal Duke wants."

Sullie didn't have a choice. She needed to hear what Duke's plans might be. She reined in her horse at the gate, turned in the saddle to face him.

"Duke needs to get control of some of the land over by his place. Needs more grazin' land for cattle he's gonna get." Dutch looked at her steadily, his voice firm and a little louder than it needed to be for her to hear.

"We don't plan to make any changes right now. He can look somewhere else for land if he needs it." She nudged her horse forward, but Dutch moved his horse ahead of her and halted.

"Little missy, don't get uppity with me. Duke has plans and this is one of 'em."

"Get out of my way. You have no more business here now. Just give Duke my answer." She nudged her horse forward, and Dutch backed away a bit.

"I'm sure you'll be hearin' from him real soon, little missy. Meanwhile, you best be careful about ridin' around alone. Never know what might happen." He leered, hacked out a cough, then turned and headed back toward Duke's.

When Brady came later, Sullie told him about the encounter and about Duke's plan to get control of some of their land. Dutch was a dangerous man, and Duke might be, too. They'd have to take precautions. The first would be to hire a reliable hand to be at the place when Sullie was there alone and to accompany her when she was riding either way between the two ranches. Brady would increase his efforts to find that person in town.

They worked at the Marsh place the rest of the afternoon, checking fence lines and water holes, clearing corrals and tending to horses. The cattle looked fine--fat and calm.

It was evening when they were ready to start toward their own place. The horses were saddled and Sullie was closing up the house when Duke rode up. His voice was sharp and aggressive when he declared, "Dutch tells me you're not willing to let me have some of that land over by my place."

Brady's jaw was firm. "That's right. We're not ready to make any changes at this time."

"Cora and me need the land, whether you're ready or not. The folks made a bad mistake when they left you in charge, and I'm gonna get that straightened out, one way or another." His look was bitter, sour, strained.

"We're not in charge of your land, Duke; only this place. You have plenty of other options besides a chunk of the main ranch. The folks were concerned about keeping the Marsh land together as much as possible. We're gonna honor that plan of theirs."

Duke's anger was so evident Brady thought he might reach for the rifle in the scabbard.

"I said, one way or another. You'd best keep an eye out." Duke jerked his horse around and galloped off.

"I'm sorry to see my family in this situation," Sullie said quietly. "I think it'll only get worse."

They rode back to their own small place, greeted Oscar, and put the horses away. Supper was quiet, and their conversation was solemn as they considered how to keep themselves safe from Duke and Dutch. And Cora as well.

* * *

Harvey was an excellent provider. They'd enjoyed fish, rabbit, prairie chicken, and quail plus wild onions, some kind of greens Brady didn't recognize, and roots resembling small turnips, which Harvey fried in lard. They'd seen deer and antelope, but that made a bigger stash of meat than they wanted to carry, and they didn't want the sound of a gunshot announcing their presence, although they hadn't seen a single person since their run-in with the homesteader.

In the late afternoon, Brady saw landforms in the distance--irregular, higher than the rolling hills they'd been riding through. He pointed it out to Harvey, questioning. Harvey grunted and said, "Badlands."

Brady realized then he'd heard of the Badlands. He'd

never been through that area; he'd never been this close before. He'd heard about the dangers of the area--no water, lots of rattlesnakes, rough land where fragile sandstone broke out underfoot; occasional outlaws holing up there--in general a bad place to be. Aptly named. The horizon seemed to change even as they rode toward it. The light made huge differences in the peaks and mesas. The whole shape of the landscape seemed to be moving, remodeling itself as darkness approached.

They'd ridden late, and it was full dark when they hobbled the horses, ate, and arranged their bedrolls. Oscar had done well again, but he seemed plumb ready to lie down next to Brady for the night.

* * *

The judge rapped his gavel and ordered, "Will the defendant rise."

Brady struggled, clumsy, to his feet, his handcuffed wrists held before him.

"Brady Quillan, a jury of your peers has found you guilty of the murder of Duke Marsh. Sentencing will take place tomorrow at nine o'clock. Do you have any words at this time?"

Brady's brain was a jumble of words: "Duke was a murderer himself! He was responsible for the murder of my wife!" "He killed my dog!" "He wounded my partner!" "He stole land and cattle from me!" "He's evil, evil, evil..." But though he struggled to speak, none of the words came out of his mouth. He felt himself groaning and choking as he tried to say the thoughts in his head. He moaned, his tongue thick in his throat.

Then he felt Harvey's hand on his arm, gently shaking him. "You worry in night again. Time to wake up. Clear you head."

He shrugged off his sleep, tried to get awake.

"Nah, Harvey. This wasn't the worry in the night. This was different. This stuff hasn't happened. It's a nightmare." He sat up, tried to clear his mind. The image of the judge in the courtroom was too real to dismiss as a dream, too real to put behind. He tried to explain it to Harvey, tried to replay the judge's stern look, his own pitiful look, handcuffed and unable to speak, but the concerns of himself in the nightmare and the very real possibility of that outcome were powerful. He wondered if this was some kind of foreshadowing, some kind of warning. Harvey was the one who would have pointed out that it was "One. Same." Maybe it was this living of it in sleep that would occur again in a few days or weeks. He'd already suffered it once. He'd maybe suffer it again...? Yes, he'd kill Duke if he had to; but these other things--Duke killing Oscar? Wounding Harvey? He had to prevent it. At all costs. The Badlands--a bad omen, maybe. But they'd push through. Prepare ahead of time. Keep a sharper watch. Get to Duke Marsh and his crooked wife. Find justice for the Marsh legacy.

Chapter 9

The territory was dangerous. Difficult, changeable without notice, extreme in temperature and layout, demanding. Rattlesnakes, prairie dog holes, steep gullies and washouts, big patches of prickly pear, long miles with no water. And, according to Harvey Two Shirts, the Badlands would be the worst of all, followed soon after by the black mountains, Paha Sapa.

Harvey was familiar with the territory and started immediately suggesting preparations that would make the trip more nearly possible. He indicated there would be a small settlement just a half day's ride before the trail would lead into the Badlands. That settlement was eventually in sight, and they would spend a little time there, replenishing supplies, resting their horses and themselves. Brady was interested to see a couple of fur traders' places on the narrow dirt road through the settlement. There was also a run-down general store and a tiny bar.

"Some of my people here," muttered Harvey. "Maybe they see Duke Marsh."

They tied their horses at the hitching post in front of the general store, and Brady went in to restock their supplies. He added a large canteen to a small collection of food stuff. Brady gathered his supplies and took them to the counter, where the owner tallied up his bill. The owner was helpful and not nosy. "We got a shower out back if yer so inclined," the old man offered. "No charge if ya clean up after yerself and use yer own towel." It was an attractive possibility. Brady packed his supplies in the saddlebags and pouches, then looked around for Harvey. No sign. He went back into the store and told the old man he'd take him up on the shower. He had his own soap and he had a couple of bandanas to dry off with. The shower stall had a dry board floor--no one had been there for quite a while. The water was in a big tub suspended above the floor, with ample room for someone even as tall as Brady. Water was regulated by a tug on the rope hanging from the tub. There was also a dipper hanging on a nail. Brady stripped off and stepped beneath the tub. The water was a little cool--but that was refreshing to him. Soaped all over, rinsed, even ran a razor over his chin a little. Tipped a little more water onto the floor to rinse the soapy scum, flapped out the bandanas, dressed in his same clothes. Felt civilized again. To a degree, at least.

Harvey was waiting for him back in front of the store. Brady draped the wet bandanas over the saddle horn and waited for Harvey to report his findings.

"My people say Duke Marsh here seven days ago. Lost much money in poker cards at bar. Try to leave with no paying. Big fight."

It was the most Brady had ever heard Harvey say at one time.

"Duke woman drunk, shoot at front of bar." Brady had noticed burlap nailed across the bottom of the front window of the bar but figured it was damage from a storm. Well, it could have been for sure a storm if Cora was involved.

"High class folks, huh?" Brady offered. "No law around to straighten them out a little?"

"No law here." Harvey sniffed the air. "You have soap on you."

"Yep. There's a shower out back. Want the soap? No cost if you don't need a towel."

"I wait for after Badlands. Plenty many dirt in Badlands."

They had lunch at the tiny bar--meat and potatoes, so Oscar would get a helping, too. Later, Brady went to a fur trader's stash and negotiated for a big deer hide. He figured if wind storms came up, the hide would help protect their meager belongings, maybe even provide some shelter. They filled all their canteens, offered the horses and Oscar all they could drink, and headed out across the prairie.

Harvey knew of a short route, cutting through just the edge of the Badlands, avoiding the rougher interior. Brady had total trust in Harvey and his knowledge of the area. In the few days of their travel, Brady had given up his resistance to Harvey's strong--almost stubborn--suggestions.

Brady's nightmare still lingered in his mind, and when he tried to think instead of developments before Sullie's death, it all seemed bleak, fated to tragedy. He was fortunate in one aspect, at least: He had been able to hire a young man to live at the Marsh place--a young man who knew the risks involved, who seemed more than capable of handling himself if Duke, Dutch, or Cora threatened him. He'd been a cavalry trooper, and he was good with both his pistol and his rifle. He had his own horse and had lived on a ranch in Wyoming before heading east. Unless there were hidden secrets of some kind in his background, he seemed a good prospect for serving as Marsh ranch manager and Sullie's occasional protector. Brady introduced him to Sullie by just his last name, Tassler.

The young cowboy tipped his hat, grinned, and said, "Most folks just shorten it to Tassle."

Sullie smiled, glad the young man seemed clean and decent, eager to get started.

They took him to the Marsh place, helped him move his few belongings into the house, establish which bedroom he'd use, showed him around the barn, and then Brady rode with him along the fence lines, pointing out watering holes and problem areas with erosion and washout. He'd already told Tassle about the problem with Duke, and he told it again, pointing out areas where Duke or his men may try to cut fences, where the Marsh cattle normally grazed. The cowboy was solemn, paid close attention to Brady's words.

Sullie was comfortable with Tassle and they soon settled into a routine where Brady rode to the Marsh place every morning. Occasionally Sullie went with him to cook for Tassle, deliver supplies, or clean the house. When she was ready to go back home, Tassle would accompany her if Brady wasn't ready to go yet. Oscar was always at the place to keep watch.

Tassle had been at the Marsh place just about two weeks before he ran into Duke in the pasture. As he told it to Brady, he had approached Duke and asked if he could be of help. Duke snarled in his usual manner and replied, "The hell you think you could do to be of help?" He spat, then wiped his arm across his mouth.

"Well, you wouldn't be over here on this land if you didn't need help, I don't reckon. Whaddya need?"

"I need you squatters offa this land. Pronto. Things'll get rough if I don't see that happenin' right away."

"I was told this is Quillan property now and you're trespassing."

"You was told wrong." Duke unsheathed his rifle. "Now git the hell outa here before I have to use this."

Tassle was no coward, could have called Duke on the threat. But he thought he should check in with Brady first, learn what action they should take. He turned his horse, headed back to Marsh headquarters.

Brady was at the house. He quickly got his horse, and the two of them headed back toward where Tassle had run into Duke. Duke was gone and there was no sight of him as far as they could see. They were a long way from Duke's place, but there were hills and gullies where a rider could slip out of view. They headed back toward the Marsh place, keeping an eye out for sign of anything out of the ordinary--and their sharp eyes paid off: A small herd of Marsh cattle were bunched in a washout, apart from the main herd. Brady and Tassle rode closer and saw that two of the cows were hurt--bloody legs and scrapes on their shoulders.

Tassle was puzzled, asked what could have caused such wounds. Brady guessed at several possibilities: Run through barbed wire, caught in traps of some kind, crashed through heavy machinery. Even deliberately slashed.

They drove the small herd back toward a little pond, pushed the two cows into the edge of the water, eased them around a bit to wash off the blood, then moved them back to the main herd. It took them a long time, and it was nearly dark when they returned to headquarters.... to find the front door of the house open--not just open but sagging on its hinges. They dismounted in a hurry, rushed inside and found the entryway and kitchen were trashed. Chairs were upturned, pots and pans strewn all over, curtains torn from the windows, cupboard doors open and canned food thrown to the floor. Farther inside, the mattress on Tassle's bed was slashed, his few clothes scattered on the floor. There didn't seem to be damage to the living room and dining room where Mrs. Marsh's things were still in place. Old Marsh's desk was still orderly, his chair in its regular position.

There was no doubt in Brady's mind who was responsible. The doubts were what to do about it.

He and Tassle straightened up as much as they could, repaired the door, and set about planning ways to avoid a repeat of the intrusion. The door wasn't usually locked; Brady would buy locks for doors and windows and they'd be installed right away. Tassle would plan sabotage for the porch and entryway. But the main thing was to keep very close watch on every approach to the ranch, to stay armed and meet every visitor with distrust.

Those were the reactions. Brady and Tassle would need to plan the proactions as well. That was a much harder proposition. Duke was family, like it or not. Brady couldn't just go threaten him with gunfire. At least not yet. Reporting the invasion to the sheriff was a possibility, but unlikely to result in any action. The final decision was to take no action immediately but to wait and see what Duke might try next--but to be prepared for anything that might occur.

* * *

As they rode toward the pink sandstone formations, Brady became more and more aware of the dangers they might face. Harvey seemed casual but alert. He insisted that Oscar ride up on the "saddle" with him--the sandstone was hot. Oscar kept a good lookout from his perch in front of Harvey. Old Horse gimped along at a good pace, and the sorrel had good energy. He'd been shod recently, so Brady didn't worry about his feet.

It wasn't long before they were riding through weird shapes--towers, flat mesas, windswept slopes, cave entrances. They saw a few rattlesnakes but no other wildlife. There seemed to be a few paths or faint trails leading off to the left, but Harvey kept heading straight west and occasionally a bit northwest. The trail was mostly level, only occasionally hilly. There was one steep rise, and at the top, Brady could see to the south a much larger area of sandstone formations; it looked impassable.

Midafternoon a light wind had started, and as they rode, it picked up. Sand blew in swirls around them; it didn't seem to be wind from any particular direction, just EVERY direction. Harvey had pulled a blanket up over his shoulders, and Brady did the same. Both had bandanas to protect their faces. Oscar hunched down into Harvey's chest, only his head peering out.

The wind increased, and Harvey pointed toward a freaky looking sandstone dome, indicating they would head in that direction. The dome resembled an overturned bowl, broken off to form a sort of shelter. There was even grass under the dome; there had to be water somewhere nearby. The wind whipped around them as they rode into the sheltered area of the dome. They unloaded Oscar, loosened cinches, hobbled horses, moved against the back wall of the bowl. They each drank from their canteens and Brady poured a drink for Oscar. The new deerskin was unrolled and spread to cover the shoulders of both men with Oscar between them, and they prepared to wait it out until the wind died down.

Even in their sheltered area, the sand stung as it was blown into their faces. The horses stood butt-end to the front of the dome and nibbled at the grass when the wind was not so violent. Oscar's nose was buried in Brady's elbow. The wind howled and moaned, sometimes almost shrieking, other times only a groan. Often it was so loud they would have had to shout to be heard, but neither spoke.

Time passed. Brady knew he had napped. Harvey had nudged him. Brady looked at him and Harvey motioned to be quiet. Brady strained to hear something over the wind, but the only sounds he could make out were just more moans and whines. Harvey stood, and Oscar stood with him. Finally Brady heard it: A voice, weak but close. He stood as well, holding his rifle at the ready. Harvey moved toward the open end of the dome, then bent low and moved toward the right, in the direction from which they had ridden. A few silent steps, and then Harvey straightened, moved quickly forward and reached down to grab a figure. Brady was right behind him.

The figure slumped, groaned, then choked out a few words. "Help. I need help. Water."

Brady and Harvey lifted and dragged the man into the sheltered area. As they propped him against the back wall, Brady saw blood on the front of the man's clothes. Harvey poured water from his canteen into a tin cup, offered it to the man. With shaking hands, the man reached for it, spilling some. Harvey steadied the cup, and the man drank.

"Who are you and what's happened to you?" Brady asked gruffly.

The man choked and groaned, then answered. "Got shot. Over east."

"How'd you get shot? And where over east?"

But the man had slumped over and didn't respond. Harvey moved in and started lifting the man's clothing to find the source of all the blood. He grunted when he found the wound--high up on the man's chest, the blood still oozing.

Brady hadn't packed much in the way of medical supplies. Harvey found a bandana and started cleaning the man's wound. Brady offered his soap, and soon the site of the wound was at least cleared of dirt and dried blood. The man only groaned and twitched, no more talk. Harvey got into one of his pouches and brought out a small bag of some kind of powder. He sprinkled a bit on the man's wound, then pressed a damp bandana over it.

"Maybe bullet still in," Harvey grunted.

Brady looked closely and pried the edges of the wound apart but couldn't see anything but chewed up, bloody flesh.

"Get your knife and we'll get it out while he's still not awake."

Harvey hesitated just a moment, then reached to his side for his knife. He wiped it with a damp bandana, then hovered over the man.

"Man maybe not good. Maybe bad."

It was certainly a possibility that the man was an outlaw. But it was also a possibility that he was a lawman. Or even just an innocent bystander in some fracas. Harvey grunted again.

"Good man hurt. Bad man hurt. It is one. Same." Harvey nodded to Brady and knelt beside the man. Brady knelt on the opposite side to be sure the man didn't move as Harvey worked on him.

Brady had dealt with human wounds as well as animal wounds, and he wasn't squeamish about what Harvey was doing. Harvey's knife was sharp, and it was only a matter of minutes until Harvey extracted the bullet. The blood was oozing freely, and Harvey sprinkled more of his powder on the open wound. They pressed another bandana on the man's chest, then tied a sleeve from his shirt around the man's chest to hold it in place.

The wind had died down. It was time for Brady and Harvey to move on. But the man was not conscious; he had no horse. It wasn't possible for the two of them to transport him. There wasn't any wood around to build a travois even if they did decide to try to move him. Hell, he might not even live for the next few hours. Brady spoke his concern aloud to Harvey. Harvey didn't respond but was soon hustling around the bundles and packs on Old Horse. He moved to the sorrel and got Brady's lariat. He tied his own lariat to Brady's, then picked up the new deerskin.

"We use."

Soon Harvey was punching holes at the edges of the deerskin. It took Brady a while to figure out what Harvey's plan was; but then it made sense. Rather than poles, Harvey would use the lariats for support, fix the deerskin across them to support the man's body, loop the ends of the lariats over the saddle horn--a less rigid but hopefully stable travois.

Brady moved to help, pulling the deerskin taut while Harvey threaded a thong through the holes. They lapped the deerskin over itself to make the bed just the width of the man's torso.

Brady had been looking at the man, trying to figure what kind of a guy he might be. Pretty young. Dark hair. Nothing special about his clothes. Boots well worn. They hadn't checked for a wallet; the less the body was moved, the better off he would be. No wedding ring. Brady fingered his own gold band and felt his guts tighten again. He shook his head, had to focus on the present.

"By the way, Harvey, what was that powder you used on this guy?"

"Good medicine."

"Yeah, but what?"

"Good medicine." And that was the end of that medical conference.

There was a problem with Harvey's make-do travois: The guy's feet would drag on the ground since the lariats weren't stiff enough to do anything with his body weight except pull it in a loose bundle. But Harvey soon brought Oscar's pie pan from Old Horse, and that would protect the guy's boots at least for a while. Using another of Harvey's leather thongs, they tied the man's boots to the pan.

"Half day to end of Badlands. Homestead there. Or maybe find wood before." It was settled. They'd drag the injured man behind them. It was the best they could do. Again they set out, headed west.

Chapter 10

It was a bumpy ride for the injured cowboy. They could travel only at a walk, to spare him even more discomfort. At least he was unconscious and unaware of his circumstances. They had stopped twice to check on him, wipe his face with a wet bandana. At the third stop, they found the man with his eyes open, squinting, his face sweaty, his mouth clamped tight.

"Where you takin' me?" The voice was weak but understandable.

"Headed west," Brady responded. "Who are you and what happened? Where were you headed?"

The man didn't answer. Harvey untied the shirt sleeve that served as a bandage, moved the stained bandana aside and inspected the wound. Brady provided another bandana, and Harvey sprinkled more of his powder on the wound. The edges of the wound were dark, slightly turned under. There was no fresh blood, no sign of infection yet. They wrapped the man's chest, and Brady asked him again for information; the questions again went unanswered.

Mounted, they continued on the trail. They had gone only a short distance before Harvey spied the wreckage of a wagon slightly off the trail. He dismounted and went quickly to rescue a piece of wood. They replaced Oscar's pie pan with the wood, leaving the man's boots with more space between them. The pie pan went back into Harvey's pouch, scraped clean on the bottom from miles of sandstone but at least not scraped completely through.

Hours later, they left the Badlands, emerging onto a flat prairie. In the distance, they could see a small homestead, and beyond that, wooded hills. They headed for the homestead, this time eager to find inhabitants rather than trying to avoid them.

The homestead was in good shape, small but well cared for. A small herd of cattle and a few horses were close by, and there were trees and a corral close to the house. Harvey motioned for Brady to go first, and they approached the house. As soon as they were within hollering distance, a man stepped out of the door. He was old, a little hunched over; he carried a gun in his left hand. They rode closer, stopped just yards from the man.

Brady nodded, then spoke in what he hoped was a respectful tone.

"Sorry to bother you, sir."

"Howdy. Looks like you might have a problem." The man squinted up at Brady as he came closer to them.

"Yeah, we have an injured man here. Need to know how far it is to help."

"What happened to him?" The man was walking toward the improvised travois, frowning.

"Gunshot. We don't know who he is or how it happened. We fixed him up the best we could, but he's in bad shape." Brady wondered if he might be giving more information than he should, but the old man didn't seem threatening, just curious.

"It's a long piece to get to a doc. There's a sheriff about twenty miles straight ahead. Might be the best bet to go there." The old man scratched his head then added, "The wife is pretty handy with wounds. Maybe you should let her take a look."

"We'd sure appreciate that," Brady said in a hurry. He stepped off his horse and moved toward the travois.

"Purty unusual rig you got there for that fella."

"We had to use what we had. Couldn't leave him where we found him." As Brady moved closer, he saw that the man was older than he first thought, seemed too thin and almost feeble. He also noticed that the wounded cowboy's eyes were still closed. "Might should have your wife come out here to look at him. Sorta hate to move him outa the travois."

"Yer right." The old man stepped toward the door, called, "Lou! Come on out here a minute!"

Almost immediately, as if she had been at the door waiting for the word, a tall, thin, elderly woman stepped out. "Howdy, boys. Needin' some help?" Her voice was strong, and she moved quickly toward the travois. "I'm Lou Jensen. Looks like you've got a serious case here."

"Yes, ma'am, looks bad. I'm Brady Quillan and this here's Harvey Two Shirts. We found this guy...well, he found us... back in the Badlands a ways. He was in bad shape, and we didn't have much to help him with."

Lou had already begun unwrapping the cowboy's bandage. "Wes, would you bring some fresh water and some clean towels?"

Wes gimped back toward the side of the house, where a pump handle stood out. He was soon back with a pail of water.

Brady knelt by the travois, tried to be of help. It was easy; the cowboy wasn't moving. The lady began swabbing the wound carefully. "This looks pretty good, not infected. Whatever you did must have been pretty effective. I'll pad this and rewrap it. He oughta be able to make it to the sheriff's office, if that's where you're headed." She looked at Brady with a question in her eyes.

"Yes ma'am, if that's what you think is best." Brady really wanted to unload this burden, but it didn't look as if this would be the best place. "Any chance you have some poles so we could make a better travois? This one's a little rough on him."

"Sure! Why sure!" Wes and Lou answered at the same time.

Wes scuffled around the back of the house and soon reappeared with two long poles, perfect for a travois. Brady and Harvey set to work quickly, moving the injured man carefully to the ground, then changing the deerskin from the lariats to the poles for a sturdier travois. While they worked, Wes watched and Lou bathed the cowboy's face and spoke gently to him. As far as Brady could tell, there was no response.

They resettled the cowboy in the repaired travois, mounted up and prepared to leave. "We sure thank you for your help. We'll get this guy to the sheriff as soon as we can." Brady tipped his hat to each, and they left the old couple looking after them as they rode.

Brady figured they had a good half day's ride to the sheriff's place. The short while they were at the Jensen's had provided a bit of rest for the horses, and they walked at a good pace. In a few places, the trail was smooth enough for them to move at a slow trot--anything to make the trip quicker.

As before, they stopped occasionally to wipe the cowboy's face, check him for fever and to see if he was still breathing. There was a small creek not far off the trail, and they watered the horses and Oscar, then got back on the trail again. It would be nightfall before they reached the sheriff's place, and Brady hoped the sheriff lived either at his office or close by.

They didn't stop to cook a meal; it was jerked beef and a slug of water. Hopefully there'd be an eating place wherever the sheriff was.

* * *

As the sky darkened, so did Brady's mood. He thought back to the last days of Sullie's short life. Both of them were tense, always on the lookout for Duke or someone from his place. They were at their own place, doing evening chores when three riders came to the gate. It was Duke, Cora, and Dutch. Duke was slightly ahead, and Brady saw them as they approached. Brady walked toward the gate, his rifle with him.

"What's on your mind, Duke?"

"Squatters, what's always on my mind." He lifted himself up slightly, bracing on the pommel of the saddle. "Just wanna let you know I'll be moving the fence line this week end. We'll be taking over the riverfront land and the rest of it up to the road."

"What are you talkin' about?! That's not your land and you won't be moving any fence!" Brady was outraged and frustrated--how could Duke even think he had the right to do that?

"I said we'll be moving the fence line." Cora looked sour and smug; Dutch simply sat on his horse, observing. Duke reined his horse around and headed out; the other two followed.

Sullie came up behind him. She had heard the whole short exchange. "I can't even believe Duke is trying this," she exclaimed. "What can we do?"

"The only thing we can do: Get Tassle over here this week end, keep our weapons handy, shoot if we have to. I don't think the sheriff will come out to help us, but if you think so, I'll ride to town tomorrow and see."

"No, I think you're right. We're on our own for this one."

* * *

It was after sunset when Brady and Harvey reached the settlement where they hoped to find the sheriff. Brady led the way into the little cluster of buildings and soon found the small office with a sign featuring a star in front of it.

Brady dismounted and walked up to the door. There was lantern light inside; he tapped on the door, then opened it and entered. A fat man sat at the desk, hat and gun taking up most of the desk's surface. His chair had squeaky rollers as he backed up in order to stand.

"Evenin'," Brady offered.

"Evenin' to you," the sheriff responded.

"We've got a man we thought you might be able to help us with," started Brady.

"Well, shore. What kinda help?"

"He's hurt. Not even conscious. And we don't know who he is."

"Well bring him in and we'll see if I can recognize him. Where'd you bring him from?"

"Badlands." Brady moved back to the door, then stepped out and asked Harvey to help him carry the travois into the sheriff's office. There was hardly enough room for the travois inside, and Brady cringed as they lowered the injured cowboy onto the floor.

"Jesus Christ! What the hell?! He don't even look alive!" The words came out in a sputter.

"He's gunshot. Does he look like anybody you know?"

"Hell, he looks like a dead guy to me. Lemme see closer." The sheriff stooped over to peer at the cowboy's face.

"Well, I'll be damned. He does look a little like one of the Norby boys. The youngest one." He squinted, moved to the other side of the travois. "Mebbe, mebbe not. They been gone from here a couple of months. Haven't seen any of 'em for a while."

"Any idea how we can contact 'em to turn this guy over

to 'em?"

"Nah, not right off." The sheriff moved back to his chair, squeaked back to his original position. "Well now wait. There's mebbe a aunt or something down the road a ways. Yeah, she's been around a long time and them boys used to hang out there some."

"Tell me which direction and we'll take him there now. We gotta get back on our own trail right away."

"Now hold on. I gotta fill out a report on this. Can't take the responsibility for a half-dead guy comin' in here and then back out." He pulled open a drawer, pulled out some printed papers and assumed a more official posture. "Now what's his name?"

"Told ya. We don't know his name. You're the one who said maybe Norby."

"Okay. Norby. Question mark. And you found him in the Badlands. Where'bouts in the Badlands?"

"He crawled up to us just off the main trail." Brady was losing patience. Harvey merely stood quietly, listening to every word.

"And when was this?"

"Day or so ago." Brady's impatience showed in his voice. The sheriff grumbled a bit, shuffled the papers, made a few notes, then handed the pages to Brady.

"Read it over, then sign it. Print your name first, then sign it."

Brady did that, then slid the papers back to the sheriff.

"He needs to sign it, too," said the sheriff, nodding in Harvey's direction. "Can he write?"

Brady had no idea, but handed the papers to Harvey. Harvey looked over the pages, then moved to the desk, picked up the pencil and wrote. Brady looked sideways at him as he wrote smoothly. Harvey handed the pages to Brady, and Brady was surprised--and pleased--almost proud--to see that Harvey's handwriting was textbook perfect--slanted evenly, every letter clear, no fancy flourishes. He handed the report back to the sheriff and asked again for directions to the aunt's house. It would be a short trip, and hopefully the end of their guardianship of the injured cowboy.

"What kind of people are these Norby folks?" Brady inquired as they lifted the cowboy to haul him back outside.

"Some are okay but most of 'em pretty rough. Haven't had one in jail in a good while, though. Helped when they moved off."

They hooked the travois up to Old Horse again and moved off to deliver their charge to the unexpectant aunt. It was plumb dark, and Brady was glad the aunt lived on the main trail out of town. He looked briefly for a sign of an eating place, but the street was dark and there were no cooking smells in the air.

There had been no movement by the cowboy the whole time they were in the sheriff's office. They had paid attention to his breathing, but that was the only sign of life.

Brady was curious. "Harvey, where'd you learn to write so well?"

"Schoolteacher lady."

"You went to school?"

"Work for her."

"And she taught you?"

Harvey didn't speak, just nodded. End of conference on Harvey's education.

It didn't take long for them to reach what they assumed was the aunt's place--a good-sized house with light in the windows. They rode up to the front, and Brady dismounted to go to the door. It was opened before he had a chance to knock.

"Hello, ma'am. Sorry to come so late, but the sheriff said you were the one we need to see."

"Well, hello to you, too. And what's your business?" Her voice was just a little cautious but still friendly.

"We have a wounded man here, and the sheriff says he's one of your kinfolk."

"Oh, my goodness! Well, let me see! Bring him in, bring him in." Her caution disappeared, and she opened the door wider. Brady moved back toward Old Horse to help Harvey with the travois. They soon had the cowboy inside, in a wide hallway. The aunt held a lantern over the travois.

"I can't tell. It might be Leon. He looks awful." Her voice weakened. "Please tell me what happened."

Brady went through the whole story for her, regretting he had no more to tell. As he spoke, she watched him intently, her eyes not leaving his face for a second. She was a middle-aged woman, pretty in a plain sort of way, clad in a long dress with an apron. Very feminine.

"And the sheriff filled out a report? "

"Yes, ma'am."

"And did you collect the reward?"

"Reward? No ma'am. No mention of a reward."

"Well, if this is Leon, there's a reward on him. And the sheriff could have verified that in the blink of an eye." She moved closer to the travois then, held the lantern over the cowboy and inspected his face carefully. "I'm so sorry he's hurt. He's a fine boy and I love him just like the rest of them. But there's a price on him. If they put him in jail he may straighten out. He's young enough to change his ways, and his mother would help him all she could."

The aunt felt the cowboy's brow, moved his head side to side, put her head to his chest. "I'd like to see his wound," she said, moving to loosen the bandage. The wound looked as it had each time Brady had seen it--purplish but not oozing blood.

"You've done well to care for him to this extent," she said. "He can stay here, of course, and I'll get word to his mother. My sister-in-law." She frowned. "He's a fine boy," she repeated, "and I think we can get him through this, one way or another. Just help me get him into a bed. Just down the hall here."

Harvey and Brady stepped quickly to the travois and followed the aunt down the hall. An iron bed stood against one wall, and it was an easy movement for the men to lift the cowboy onto the bed. His clothes were filthy, and Brady cringed to see him on the white bedding.

"Now I thank you for the care you've given him. You've obviously saved his life--or at least extended it. Now...I think you need to go back by the sheriff's office and get him straightened out about the reward." She clucked a little. "Nobody ever said Sheriff Grandle was the most honest man on earth. He prob'ly figured Leon would be dead by morning, probably meant to arrange for one of his pals to claim the reward and then split it with him."

"I don't know," Brady protested. "We signed some papers in his office..."

"Hah. Papers can get lost. Just go on back by there and claim the reward. It's not much, but it might help you on your way. It's fair enough payment for your saving him." She flapped her apron and moved with them toward the door. "You might think it's strange I want you to claim the reward. But this is how it is: I want him jailed so we can start getting him straightened out."

Brady adjusted his hat. "We'll drop in on the sheriff. And good luck taking care of your nephew. He looks in pretty bad shape." He and Harvey stepped toward their horses. "Do you mind if we leave the travois poles here? We'll take the deerskin, but it'd be handy if we didn't have to tote the poles."

"Sure, sure. Whatever you need. Matter of fact, let me fix you a quick bite to eat. You're probably hungry."

"We sure appreciate that, ma'am." Brady and Harvey went outside to dismantle the travois, and the aunt stepped through a doorway into what must have been a kitchen. By the time Brady and Harvey were through taking the travois apart and packing the deerskin, the aunt stepped through the door and handed them a small package.

"It's just meat and biscuits," she said. "But maybe it'll fill an empty spot for you. And thank you again for helping Leon." It was a dismissal, and Brady and Harvey mounted and moved off toward the sheriff's office.

It was a few minutes down the trail when Brady exclaimed, "We don't even know that lady's name!"

"Norby."

"Well, that's the cowboy's name, but what about hers?"

"Norby on gatepost."

"Oh. Glad you noticed. Well, let's get on to the sheriff. Reward. Hmmm. That's a switch." They moved into a trot and the trip back to the sheriff's office was a quick one.

They pulled up in front of the little building and were glad to see there was still light in the windows. They dismounted and Brady was headed for the door when he felt Harvey's hand on his arm.

"Huh? What?"

"You need reward money?"

"Well, no. I 've got enough to get us to the mining camp and back. Why do you ask?" He paused a moment, then added, "I just don't want the crooked sheriff to get it."

As usual, Harvey grunted and waited before answering. "We help man. Aunt help man. It is one. Same. But not same."

"What do you mean, Harvey?"

"We help man one day. Aunt help man many days."

"Yeah, that's true."

"Maybe tell sheriff reward go to aunt. Then we go for Duke Marsh. Catch him fast."

Brady's admiration of Harvey increased. "That's a good idea. We'll make sure the sheriff knows he has to pay Mrs. Norby. I may need to write the local judge a letter to be sure that happens, but we'll start by just telling the sheriff what he needs to do."

Brady pushed the door open, startling the fat man. "We're just checking in to let you know we delivered the Norby boy to his aunt, as you authorized us to do." He emphasized the last phrase. "Now we're telling you that instead of giving us the reward, you'll be giving it to Mrs. Norby."

The sheriff sputtered, coughed, cleared his throat, squeaked his chair back and forth. "Uh, well..."

"I'll be contacting the judge to be sure he knows this is what's being done, and I'm sure he'll be in touch with you."

The sheriff puffed, blanched a little, then shuffled the papers on his desk. "There'll be more paperwork, of course, but, yes, uh...er...I can take care of that. Yes...uh...Mrs. Norby. Right."

Harvey and Brady made it back through the door in quick time. Poor Oscar had been glad for the brief rest, having kept up with all the events of the past long hours. They'd find a campsite soon where the three of them and the horses would all rest up before hitting the real trail again in the search for Duke and Cora Marsh. It had been an unavoidable break in their routine, but they'd make good progress again the next day.

Chapter 11

Campsite. Horses hobbled. Frybread. Bedrolls out. Quiet night. Early morning coffee, more frybread. Brady wouldn't get tired of it, and neither would Oscar.

Cool morning. They set out at a good pace, glad to be able to go at a lope now they didn't have the travois. They were approaching hills with patches of heavy cedar growth, and the trail was steeper at times.

Midmorning, they came upon a widening in the trail, a homesite off to the right. Like others they'd passed, it was small. They could pass it without much of a change in direction and still not come too close. They were about even with the little cabin when they heard a commotion.

"Suffer and die, you lowdown sonuvabitch!" This, accompanied by the sound of blows. A couple of loud thwacks, then more shouting. "You goddamn crook! You thief!" More thuds. The voice was female--loud, but definitely female.

Brady looked at Harvey, questioning. Harvey sighed, then nodded, resigned. They reined toward the cabin and soon saw a tiny little woman wielding a short-handled shovel, pounding, determined, on a huddled figure on the ground.

"You tried to kill my hen, you worthless piece of manure!" she shrieked, continuing the punishment.

The men looked at each other, mystified as to what the best procedure might be. Brady rode closer; Harvey stayed a bit behind.

"Ma'am? Can we be of help?"

"I got it, thanks. I got it just fine. The worthless sonuvabitch came in here and caught one of my hens. He was gonna EAT her!!" At this, she began a new round of pounding, with even more force.

"Ma'am, I think you've got him stopped now. I think he knows you mean it."

The little lady stood straight, wiped a stray lock of hair from her face, leaned on the shovel handle and looked squarely at Brady. "I can't abide a thief. And I can't abide a crook who'll kill a ..... a....a HEN!" She puffed and blew another lock of hair from her forehead. The man lay, groaning, on the ground. Blood came from several parts of his body, soaking through his shirt and coloring his hair.

"Does he have a horse here? How did he get here?" asked Brady.

"Hell, he lives here part of the time," answered the lady, in a calmer tone. "Well, he DID, until he pulled this stunt. I ain't having no crook or killer here on this place." She kicked a tiny foot at the bloody man.

Brady stepped toward the man, aiming to check the extent of his injuries. At least the man was conscious; this was definitely a step up from their last encounter with an injured cowboy.

"Ma'am, let's get him on a horse and get him outa here so you can get back to your...regular routine."

"He ain't gonna take a horse a mine. He can walk on home. He's through here." The lady sniffed and stuck her little jaw out.

Harvey helped Brady lift the man to a sitting position. That made his condition look a little better. The shovel wounds were fairly superficial, no real deep cuts. He would have some real visible bruises, but he'd survive.

"Sir, you're gonna have to leave now. You walk to wherever you're going, and don't come back here until the lady gives her permission." Brady's voice was firm.

The lady stomped her foot and glared at Brady. "You don't need to be givin' no orders around here, you drifter. I can handle it just fine." She turned back to the man on the ground. "You're gonna have to leave now. You walk to wherever you're going, and don't come back here until I say so." She gave a sharp nod of her head and stuck her jaw out even farther. "Git on NOW!"

Chastened, Brady tipped his hat to the lady and said, "We'll be heading on now, ma'am. Sorry you had this little problem, but, like you say, you seem to have it under control." The lady gave a modified snort and shuffled back toward her cabin, giving only one quick look backward to be sure the guilty man was heading out.

Harvey was eager to hit the trail, and Brady was eager to follow. Oscar, somewhat befuddled, took one look back but then followed the sorrel and Old Horse back to the main trail. No accounting for some folks, his disgusted look seemed to say.

A short while down the trail, Harvey muttered, "Ballard."

"What? What's that?"

"Ballard. Name."

"You mean the little lady's name is Ballard?"

"On fence post."

"Oh. Glad you noticed. We sure don't wanna cross her again any time soon."

* * *

The day went smoothly. Such fine weather, such pretty terrain. Brady looked ahead to the dark, dark hills ahead.

"Paha Sapa," said Harvey.

Brady knew that was sacred land to the Sioux, and he knew that the mining camps were encroaching on that land. Gold was the lure. Irresistible. But what was the lure for Duke? He wasn't a miner. Why would he head for the mining camps? There might be one answer: The camps were crowded; no one was paying attention to identities. That would be attractive to Duke. Also, there would be down-and-outs who would be available for a price to do almost anything. Make that just plain anything.

At that thought, Brady's mind went immediately to the reason for Duke's need for such.

* * *

Tassle came late Friday afternoon but there was no sign of trouble. He came again Saturday morning, armed and alert. The three--Brady, Tassle, and Sullie--worked in the barn and corral, keeping a sharp eye out for anything unusual. Sullie had gone into the house to start a pot of stew when Tassle caught a glimpse of movement across the pasture. "Brady! Look over yonder!"

There were three figures riding toward the far fence line. They weren't close enough for Brady to see their features, but he was certain of the identity: Duke, Dutch, and Cora. Brady grabbed his rifle and shot into the air, knowing the sound would carry across the pasture.

The figures halted, then changed direction to head toward Brady's place. Sullie had come out of the house at the sound of gunshot. Brady explained that his intention was just to stop the trio from cutting any fence. "You'd best stay inside, just in case they come this way. But keep your gun handy, too. We may need you to use it."

It took Duke and his companions quite a while to cross the pasture, come onto the road, and head toward the entry gate to Brady's ranch. In the meantime, Tassle and Brady checked their arms, made sure they were loaded and that additional ammunition was close by. Brady was tense, reluctant to have this confrontation. Tassle seemed at ease but watching closely. They continued their work in the corral, staying close to the open gate so they could move toward the entry in a hurry.

It seemed the wait was way too long, that Duke and the others were too slow in coming. It was cool, but Brady's forehead and neck were sweaty. He had his hat pulled low so there would be no glare from the sun as he watched the three approach.

They finally reached the gate, and Brady walked toward them, Tassle just behind and to the side. "Whaddya doin' here on my property?"

"I told you I was moving fence today. That's the way it is." Duke moved to reach for his pistol.

"Don't do it, Duke. No guns." Dutch had also lifted a sixgun and Cora raised her rifle from the scabbard.

"You don't tell me nothin', squatter," snarled Duke. Suddenly, his pistol had cleared the holster and he shot toward the corral, not aiming at either Brady or Tassle but warning them.

"No! No guns!" Brady moved back toward the corral, Tassle still beside him.

"I'll do what it takes, Quillan. Yer outa here, one way or another." Duke's voice was raspy, evil.

At that moment, Sullie came out of the house, looking toward Brady and Tassle.

Brady yelled quickly, "No, Sullie, get back inside!"

Sullie looked at him with a question in her eyes. He started toward her, trying to reach her, to urge her back into the house, to protect her. And suddenly, the shot rang out and echoed between the buildings. Sullie fell sideways with no sound. Blood all over. Brady couldn't move, couldn't make his brain understand what had just happened.

Tassle was stunned, too, but moved toward the three intruders with his pistol drawn. He shot quickly, but hit only Dutch's arm. The three reined backward, then whirled and spurred off. Tassle shot again and again, the shots wide and harmless. He came back slowly to Sullie's body. Brady was still standing, unmoving, a short distance away. Tassle knelt beside Sullie. Then he looked up at Brady.

"Christ, Brady. She's gone. She's gone." He moved her body a bit to straighten it, to make her look as if she had some life again. Then he rose and moved to Brady, put an arm around his shoulder and stood with him quietly. He heard Brady gulp, then an agonized cry came out. "Sullie. Sullie."

* * *

It was a horrible time. Tassle rode to town to report to the sheriff; Brady began digging a grave, just beyond the corral, with a view toward the river, toward the land Sullie bought from her father. His feeling of disbelief didn't leave him, and he knew he wouldn't be able to place her body in the grave. It couldn't be true, it couldn't be the end of Sullie. And although the sight of her lying on the ground was gruesome and horrible, he couldn't bear to cover her with a blanket. The ache inside him was worse than anything he'd ever felt--a physical pain reaching every part of him. Nausea swept over him in waves, and he used the effort of digging to keep it under control. He was still at the job when Tassle returned.

"Tassle. Who....who was it....that..?"

"Sorry, Brady. I musta been lookin' at you or Sullie. I didn't see who fired. I can't believe it, but I didn't see it." Tassle looked at the ground, shook his head.

"But you got one of them, right?"

"Yeah, I got Dutch in the arm, but I missed with the other shots."

Brady heaved a big sigh, then went back to his ineffective digging. "You got to the sheriff?"

"Yeah, they'll be out soon to look around. And they'll go to Duke's, I'm sure. They know who's responsible."

The sheriff did come and brought two other men with him. They spoke briefly with Brady, inspected the grounds, respectfully examined Sullie's body, then headed for Duke's place.

Weakness and exhaustion settled over Brady. He stumbled to the steps of the house and sat, looking bleak and worn. Tassle joined him, spoke quietly. "I'll go over to the other place and do chores. But I'll come back to help and to spend the night here.' He cleared his throat, then looked straight at Brady. "I can help you take care of Sullie. We can do it together."

"No need for that but do what you want." Brady's voice was weak, almost a whisper.

Tassle got his horse from the corral and left, leaving Brady alone with his grief--and with total disbelief that the events could have occurred. He was still sitting on the steps when the sheriff and his men came back. The sheriff had found the wounded Dutch Heisler, had questioned him relentlessly until Dutch had provided the information he wanted: Dutch said it must have been Duke who had fired. It was sudden and had caught him unaware. Cora's rifle would have been closer to him and he would have heard that more distinctive sound. Duke and Cora were not at their ranch. They had packed up and gone quickly, leaving Dutch and Dan in charge of their place. There were enough hired hands to keep the place in order. They'd be in touch at a later time.

Dutch's wound wasn't life threatening--painful, but not

crippling. The sheriff reported that Dutch was quiet, not the aggressive bully he normally was. The sheriff would alert other law enforcement officers to arrest Duke and Cora wherever they might light. The charge would be murder. Later, perhaps, this would be comforting to Brady; but for now, it only made his pain worse. Sullie. Murder. It was impossible.

Chapter 12

They had been fortunate in their days of travel. The weather had not been extreme, there had been no prairie fires, no hail storms. Their horses had stayed fit; Oscar made it along just fine with an occasional lift from Harvey. There had been prairie grass for the horses, and Harvey was a good cook. Brady's store of jerked beef was still adequate, and there were some other dried foodstuffs they ate as they rode.

Brady had no plan for when they found Duke Marsh. He knew only that they had to find him; kill him or bring him in for trial, it made no difference to Brady which. Justice for Sullie is all he had in mind. Payback. Punishment. Revenge. Whatever it might be called. As for Cora--she was evil, too. Greedy, apparently totally bound to Duke, with no conscience whatsoever. Brady knew Harvey would be supportive of any course of action Brady might take; moreover, Harvey would probably make firm suggestions.

It would take them only a few more days to make it to the mining camps. The weather should hold; no freezing temperatures for a couple of weeks yet. They would try to avoid contact with people on the trail; they couldn't risk any more delays like the thieving homesteader, the wounded cowboy or even the feisty little woman. Brady shook his head at the recollection of that little whirlwind of a female. Ballard, her name was, according to Harvey. She seemed to have more than enough of what it took to make it alone on the prairie. Good luck to her.

They were fortunate, also, that they'd had no recent confrontation with outlaws or thieves intent on stealing their gear or Brady's stash of cash. He kept it in different places-- some in his pocket, some stuffed beneath the saddle horn in the space between the saddle and the saddle blanket, some in his saddle bags. He felt fortunate that he had enough money to accomplish what he was determined to do and then to return home. He trusted Tassle to take good care of the ranch. He had to trust Tassle. It would be a good while before he could make it home.

Two uneventful days on the trail. The terrain was steadily becoming hillier, but the trail was well marked. Hopeful miners had made their way in droves, apparently, heeding the call of rich strikes in the Black Hills. Harvey rode silently except for his peculiar humming. Brady was accustomed now to the lack of conversation, stopping himself from pointing out the obvious, avoiding idle comments. There was comfort in their quiet companionship, and his appreciation of Harvey grew day by day.

Just before dawn, Brady was awakened by the sound of moving animals. He stirred, checked to see where Harvey was. Saw him standing by the horses, looking into the darkness.

"What is it, Harvey?"

"Horses come."

Brady came up to join Oscar and Harvey. "Maybe just miners heading toward the camps?"

Harvey didn't answer, just kept watching for movement in the dark. Oscar seemed intent as well, bristled and alert. Brady felt he had fewer senses than either of the other two, not hearing or seeing anywhere near as well as they could. Minutes passed. Harvey moved to begin packing Old Horse, and Brady followed suit. Hobbles removed, horses saddled and bridled, packs secured. They were ready to move out, even though it was plumb dark.

Suddenly Harvey stood stone still. "Get gun."

Brady already had his Winchester close at hand, but he lifted it to his side. "What is it?"

Again Harvey didn't answer but nodded to the east. Brady strained to hear or see. Nothing yet. Oscar rumbled a quiet growl. Then Brady saw them: Two mounted men with a pack horse, moving at a walk, headed straight for them. Harvey nodded to him, with an abrupt side movement. Brady interpreted quickly and spoke loudly through the darkness to the men.

"Hold it!"

The men reined in. "Hello the camp!"

"Yeah. Why are you off the trail?"

Neither of the men answered for a moment. The saddles squeaked as they changed position. The pack horse shuffled to the side, lowered his head to try to reach grass.

"Well, I guess we just lost the trail there for a while. Didn't mean to intrude." There was a pause, then "We could use some coffee and breakfast if you can spare."

"No coffee or breakfast here. You best be movin' on." Brady cocked his Winchester.

"We been ridin' all night. Need a break." The speaker nudged his horse forward; the other man and the pack horse followed.

"Don't come any closer. We'll be movin' on soon and you can have this campsite. But stay where you are until we leave."

"No need to rush," the man said in a louder tone. "Matter of fact, you stay right where you are." There was the sound of leather, metal against leather: the sound of a gun being drawn.

"You're covered by two guns. Better think this through." Brady's voice was hard as stone. There was no light, but he was sure the two men could see his Winchester, pointed right at the one in front. Harvey was poised for attack with knife and gun at the ready. Oscar, too, was ready, his lips pulled back in a quiet snarl.

The front man appeared to start a move to the side but suddenly fired his pistol. Brady fired the Winchester as a reflex and the man faltered in his saddle, then fell. Harvey lunged forward toward the other man, jerked him from his saddle and held his knife at the man's throat. The man cried out. "No! No, don't do it! Don't do it!" Harvey didn't move, his hand still holding the man's shirt.

"We'll tie him, Harvey." The man Brady shot hadn't moved on the ground. Brady nudged him with his foot. The man didn't respond. Brady reached to his own saddle and got his lariat. While Harvey held the man firmly, Brady tied his hands behind his back, then jerked him upright. They shoved him toward a tree, then bound him, neck and ankles, to it.

Brady got his face close to the man and growled. "Wha'd

you have in mind, comin' in here in the dark?"

The man appeared frightened. Gulped, then answered. "Just what Russ said. Lookin' for a break."

"Lookin' for what else?" Bady spoke louder this time.

"Nothin' else. Just tired. Hungry. Rode all night."

"Your pal might be dead. You might be, too, soon, if you don't answer me right."

"I got nothin' more to say. I ain't knowin' Russ for long. Can't take no blame for him." The man gulped again, winced as the rope chafed his throat.

Brady stepped away, and he and Harvey went to the downed man. Brady reached to turn him over, saw blood staining the man's shirt. He leaned low to listen for breathing. None. Felt the man's wrist for pulse. None.

"Well." Brady straightened, adjusted his hat. "Killed my first man. I don't feel too bad about it. He was up to no good." He looked at Harvey. "What do you think?"

Harvey had no comment.

Brady adjusted his hat again, moved to lift the man's feet, began dragging him into the brush. "I figger I had no choice. Self defense. I'm not worried about the law. I'll just drag him over here outa sight and we'll move out."

Harvey stepped to help him. "You kill him. The law kill him. It is one. Same."

It was strange. Brady felt no remorse. There was no feeling of guilt, no pang of conscience. Also, no blood thirst. He had no urge to do more damage to the body of the dead man, no urge to shoot the other intruder. The shot from his Winchester seemed just like a natural reaction... to preserve his own life, to protect himself, Harvey, and Oscar.

"Harvey, what do you think? About this other guy?"

Harvey shrugged.

"Maybe let him go? Or does he need...haychaydu?"

Harvey went to the packhorse, inspected the supplies. They were few.

"Haychaydu maybe done. He learn. Maybe."

Brady agreed. They untied the man, and Brady led him

to his horse, handed him the lead rope to the pack horse.

"You get the hell outa here and don't try thieving any more. You're lucky you got your life."

The man said nothing, mounted his horse. Brady took the bridle off the horse ridden by the other man, flopped it over the mound of supplies on the packhorse. "This horse'll probably follow you. And don't stop any time soon."

The man still didn't speak, just reined his horse back toward the trail and moved out at a quick trot.

* * *

Brady knew they'd be meeting more travelers as they neared the mining camps. He didn't want conversation with any of them yet. Later, when they were at the camps, he'd begin asking around for information about a couple, man and woman, traveling together. He couldn't imagine very many women in the mining camps; too rough.

It was daylight when they left the site of their rough experience with the intruders. Harvey seemed unaffected by the events. Harvey was apparently unaffected by almost any event. He just absorbed it in his quiet, stoic manner and rarely commented.

The trail had become a well-worn path, then a road. They passed abandoned gear and broken-down wagons, an occasional carcass of a game animal and once, a dead horse. The hills became low mountains, and there were a few rough buildings clustered along the road. They stopped in what seemed like a make-do general store and Brady replenished their food supplies and bought socks for each of them. Harvey immediately exchanged his holey ones for the new ones, tossed the old into a pile of trash beside the store. It interested Brady that Harvey even wore socks inside his worn moccasin-style boots. He would have thought it would be bare feet next to the deer hide. Not always easy to figure Harvey Two Shirts.

It seemed as if they were in a town, in Brady's opinion. Tents, fragile wooden buildings, pens, fences--it became more crowded as they rode. Some of the tents were clustered close together, side by side. A few horses were picketed in some open areas, and there were pack mules in several places. There weren't many people around; apparently they were panning or digging for gold, either close by or at a distance. It was hard for Brady to figure what was so attractive about this whole urge these men seemed to have.

They kept riding, in higher and rougher land. The tents became a little more scattered, but it still seemed crowded to Brady. He was sure Harvey felt the same way, and Oscar stayed very close to the sorrel as they rode. It was late afternoon when Harvey, who rode ahead, pulled up and looked at Brady with a question in his eyes.

"Yeah, we can stop anywhere near around here." Brady was a little reluctant to halt. It meant he'd have to concentrate on his search for Duke more intensely, he'd have to question miners, he'd have to prepare for the final confrontation. It was a weird, many-sided situation: Eager to find Duke, tense about what that meeting might entail, fearful of the danger for Harvey and Oscar, what the whole thing might bring down on them as far as the law was concerned. They had crippled a man, killed a man. He felt the worry of it in his gut; but he also felt a charge of energy. He was close to the end of it.

Chapter 13

Harvey cleared a small piece of ground for them--room for the horses and room for their bedrolls. It was easy to find rocks to border their fire pit, since the whole place was rocks. Brady had bought a small slab of beef at the little market. That and wajapi made a feast. And--luxury!--Brady had also bought a can of peaches. Smooth, sweet, a bit tangy--perfect! Harvey grunted in appreciation. Oscar was satisfied with his strip of beef and his frybread. He grunted as he stretched out between the bedrolls.

They were sitting quietly, enjoying their coffee when a man approached them. Brady figured him for a miner, certainly not a lawman; he had soggy boots and his pants were wet at the bottom. Oscar pricked his ears and raised his nose but didn't object to the visitor.

"Evenin' to ya, there." The man's voice was gravelly, muffled a bit by scruffy facial hair.

"Evenin'."

"Smelled yer coffee. Got any extra?"

"Got yer own cup?"

"Yep, sure do." The man pulled a tin cup from an outer pocket of his loose jacket.

Harvey poured the man a full cup, and Brady moved a little to the side to provide room for the man to sit. "Yer welcome to sit a spell if you like."

"Thanks. I'll do that." The man grunted as his lowered himself to the ground, holding his coffee carefully. He reached a hand toward Brady, mumbled, "Name's Jasper Watts. Good of ya to spare the coffee." The coffee was hot, and he sipped carefully. "Ain't had no coffee fer several days. Ain't been down to the settlement."

Brady ignored the opportunity to introduce himself and Harvey, instead poking the fire and pouring himself another splash of coffee. "You been here long?"

"Purty good while. Had good luck at first, but it's been poor lately." Jasper took another sip. "Gittin' real crowded, too."

He looked first at Brady, then at Harvey. "You plannin' to pan or dig?"

"Not either one, I don't guess," answered Brady. "Just sorta lookin' around, maybe trying to get up with somebody."

"Oh yeah? Ya got kin or partners here?"

Brady was reluctant to divulge their full mission, not knowing whether Jasper could be of help or not, not wanting to advertise their purpose. He looked at Harvey for his opinion. Harvey made a slight sideways nod.

"Nope. Just takin' stock of what's here. Might move on back down and stick around the settlement for a while."

It was quiet for several minutes except for the rustle of clothing as they raised and lowered their cups.

"Some rough folks around, but most of 'em right close here are good. Tired, mostly broke, but good." Jasper coughed, spit over his shoulder, took the last sip of coffee. He stood, slapped the cup against his leg, and stepped away from the fire. "Thanks again for the coffee. Good luck to ya."

Neither Brady nor Harvey stood as Jasper shuffled toward the path. "Heard they're hittin' it big farther west. I might head that way m'self." Those were Jasper's parting words

They watched until they could not see him anymore. Harvey turned to Brady. "He look for something."

Brady was startled; he hadn't thought anything odd about a stranger approaching their camp. If Harvey felt something, it would pay to think more about it. Jasper hadn't seemed surprised to find them camped there. In fact, the more he thought about it, Brady felt Jasper had maybe deliberately chosen their camp. He had looked them over carefully as he sat by the fire. His questions had seemed harmless, but Jasper now knew they were looking for someone, not here for the gold. What could his purpose have been? No one knew Brady and Harvey were tracking Duke and Cora. Or had Duke somehow learned they were on his trail? Jasper was down and out, probably hoping that watching the trail and reporting on who might be coming down it could earn him a little money. But Harvey had questioned Jasper's coming to their camp; that alone made Brady sure they should be cautious when they reached the settlement.

They rolled out their bedrolls but neither man went to sleep quickly. Questions of what they might find in the settlement pushed sleep away. Even Oscar seemed restless.

By sunup they had eaten frybread and jerky, given Oscar his share, and were ready to set out. The sun was getting up toward noon when they neared the mining settlement. Brady paused for a minute to look it over. It was the same as most mining settlements--hastily built because men were more interested in getting to the gold. There was a main road leading down the middle, businesses on both sides. Behind them were some houses, some a little better constructed, most not much more than single-room shanties. But men looking to get rich quick didn't worry about their lodging. Brady could see the livery stable, a boarding house, at least a couple of saloons. There was a small diner, a blacksmith, and several other businesses. A few had outhouses behind or to the side of them. Brady noticed a sheriff's office down the street.

The settlement was teeming with wagons and riders. They filled the main road, heading in and out of town. Wagons pulled by mules, riders on horses, and lots of people on foot added to the air of business going on and no time for anyone to stop. The faint jangle of a piano coming from one of the saloons could be heard over the creaking of wagons. The porches and sidewalks were filled with men and a few women. Most of the men appeared to be miners; only a few cowboys were in the crowd.

Brady and Harvey headed toward the livery stable first. They needed to get stalls for their horses and get them fed and watered. Oscar was limping and would welcome some rest; he could stay in the stalls with the horses. An old man came out of the door as they approached. He walked with a slight limp, smiled as they came close.

"Howdy, fellas, get on down." He held out his hand as Brady got off the sorrel. "My name's Zach. Ma named me Zachariah but nobody needs that much name. What kin I do for you fellas?"

Brady shook his hand and smiled in return. "Brady Quillan. And this here's Harvey Two Shirts. You got stalls and feed? And we'll leave the dog here with the horses. He's no bother to anybody."

Zach turned to go in the door. "C'mon along. Got just the thing you need." He led them through the barn to the back where there were stalls that each opened into a little pen. "Just the thing for your ponies. They can stretch their legs a little if they want. The dog can bed down here in front or in one of the stalls. They can drink out of that trough. The pump is right by it; you can fill it if they need more water."

Brady smiled to himself. Zach liked to talk; he could be a good source of information about the town and people. "Looks mighty busy around here. People doing good up at the mines?"

"The mine hit a big lode, it's doing okay," Zach replied. "But them fellas that are working on their own, lot of them have gone bust. Heard there was a big strike out west, quite a few heading that way now."

They finished unsaddling and putting the horses in stalls, got Oscar a bowl of water. Harvey quietly slipped him a piece of jerky, then the two walked with Zach out of the barn. Up the street, coming from the direction of the mine, they saw a couple of miners slowly leading a mule with something draped over its back. As they got closer, Zach exclaimed, "What the hell, that's Jasper on there!"

Brady and Harvey looked more closely at the body loaded on the mule. Same worn clothing that all the miners wore, pants legs and boots still damp. Brady wanted more confirmation about the identity. He stepped to the body. The lump of a tin coffee cup bulged from the shirt on the corpse, its handle protruding from the dusty pocket. No more doubt: This was the body of Jasper Watts.

"What's goin' on, Bart? What happened to him?" Zach shouted as he looked from one to the other of the miners. "Was he shot?"

Bart was leading the mule, and he stopped in front of the livery stable at Zach's question. "Don't know for sure, but know

Jasper here had some kinda run-in with that Marsh fella." He sighed, took a deep breath and continued. "That Marsh is big and mean and didn't seem none too pleased to see Jasper. Not till Jasper was waving his arms like a wild man and telling him something. Well, then Marsh seemed pleased. But when he started to walk away, Jasper started hollering at him. Marsh turned around and they argued some. Jasper said one last thing and Marsh shot him." He sighed again. "Damn shame."

Bart nodded toward the man leading the mule with the body. "Luke and I are headed to the sheriff's office, then we'll take Jasper to the undertaker." Luke leaned against the mule. "Heard somebody say it sounded like they were arguing about money, that Jasper was yelling that Marsh owed him. Just made Marsh madder."

Zach shook his head slowly as Bart and Luke started down the street. "That fella better git outa town quick as he can. Jasper was well liked. He was a good old boy, never got rich like he wanted but would lend a hand any time you needed one. Lots of these prospector always right behind the next big strike, never quite get there in time. Mostly they're real good folk just havin' bad luck. They won't take kindly to Marsh killing Jasper."

Brady and Harvey were stunned by the turn of events. They had confirmation now that Duke was here, and they knew now that Duke was aware they had arrived.

"Where does this Marsh guy stay?" Brady asked.

"Him and his woman used to have a shack behind the Big Strike Saloon at the other end of town. They hung out in the saloon a lot." Zach seemed to enjoy telling all he knew about what went on in town.

Brady and Harvey started down the street in the direction Jasper had been taken. Brady's mind was full of questions and plans. It would be good to know if Duke and Cora were still in town or if they had already started running. He figured the news of the killing might have already spread all over town and someone might know Marsh's whereabouts. But there was lots of violence in town; maybe the sheriff and the townspeople just sort of brushed off Jasper's killing. If there might be a chance

Duke and Cora were still in town and could be found, Brady would have to make a decision: Did he want to confront Duke and kill him, or did he want to see him punished by the law? Would it be the justice and revenge he wanted to see Duke in prison? And what about Cora? She was not the one who fired the fatal shot, so what should be done with her? How would the law handle her part in the killing of Sullie and Jasper and whatever else they may have been involved in?

Brady had no answers; he just knew that first they had to find Duke and let events play out. Harvey listened to Brady's musings silently, making no comment and asking no questions until it was apparent Brady's thoughts were winding down.

"Sheriff maybe look for Duke. We maybe find first. Better," Harvey said. "He maybe get away if sheriff find." Brady agreed; they must look quickly and find Duke if he might still be in town. If not, they would listen to the talk; somebody might be talking about the killing, somebody would know which way Duke went.

Brady suddenly felt calm, almost peaceful. He knew he had made the decision. When they found Duke, they would give him the chance to surrender and be turned over to the sheriff. If he chose to fight, he would be killed. Brady didn't even notice that he had straightened his shoulders as he began walking purposefully toward the saloon.

Harvey looked at him. "Good. He die with gun. Or die with jail."

Brady looked at Harvey for a long moment. Harvey's ability to know what he was thinking still surprised him. Harvey gave Brady the hint of a rare smile. "Him pay. Me, you get him. Eyopehyah. Punish."

They headed toward the saloon and joined the men going in and out. Harvey sat on the bench by the door, tipped his hat slightly over his eyes and appeared to be trying to nap. No one would pay any attention to him, and chances were good he would hear useful information. Brady went inside. He planned to drift around and listen in on the talk. There would be someone who knew more than others and would welcome the chance to share all he knew with somebody new. Brady knew all he would have to do would be ask a few careful questions to get all the details on what had happened at the mine, what they all thought about Duke, and where Duke might have headed.

One miner was talking loud and fast, gesturing wildly with his hands. Brady moved over beside him, listening carefully to the story. The miner didn't notice the stranger at first. When he glanced Brady's way, Brady smiled and said, "Howdy. Just got to town. You talking about that shooting up at the mine? I'll be darned--you saw it!"

The miner turned, smiled, and stuck out his hand. They shook hands, and he launched into a new telling of the shooting, probably adding more details as he thought of them. "Oh yeah, I was there. Let me tell you, it was somethin'." Brady listened carefully. He soon learned that after Jasper's body had been taken to the sheriff's office, the sheriff started looking around town for Duke. Jasper would be buried soon in the town cemetery. The miner stopped to take a big drink of his beer, and Brady took the opportunity to ask another question. "Man, that must have been something to see. But what has become of the Duke Marsh guy? Is he still around, or did he take off?" The miner was delighted to share everything he knew with this new audience. Brady listened carefully to sort out what sounded accurate and what might have been the miner's imagination making the story better.

"Well, last I saw of Duke Marsh it looked like he was headed back to town. Probably pick up that woman of his-- quite a looker, by the way. The best way to get out of town and nobody know it would be southwest. Big strikes off to the west, so he wouldn't go that way. Maybe north, but more action up that way, too, so no, probably not north."

Once he'd started answering questions, the miner couldn't keep from telling everything he knew. Brady smiled to himself. He was sure the information about big strikes and trails was fairly accurate.

Brady began to drift away as the miner turned to order another beer. He nodded to Harvey, who followed him onto the street.

"It doesn't sound like anyone knows for sure where Duke is. The sheriff's looking around here in town, but he probably wouldn't go far outa town. I think that old miner was right. Duke has most likely headed southwest to avoid the mines and any new strikes out west. Looks like it's up to us to take care of him."

"You know," Brady went on, "I think they'll be heading for a place with more people, sorta get lost in a crowd. They could be hard to find in a big town--Cheyenne or Gillette, maybe Casper. Denver is a long way beyond that, and there are mighty big mountains beyond there if they keep moving. We need to catch them before they get too far."

Harvey looked at him for a moment, then nodded. "Find Duke. End of trail."

Brady had found himself bothered by the commotion in the settlement. It was hard to sleep with drunken noise from the saloons, and the general activity always seemed to need attention. He yearned for the quiet campsites he and Harvey had pitched on their way this far. He was eager to get out of town, back on the trail. Their accommodations at the livery were pretty bleak, although Zach was a nice enough fellow, and it was handy to get news of what was going on around them.

They went quickly to the general store to add a few more essentials since there was a good chance they wouldn't find another settlement for a while. Brady made sure to get extra jerky for Oscar and threw in some streaked meat for himself and Harvey. It would last several days before going bad.

When they came out of the general store, Brady stood quietly for a few minutes. He looked thoughtfully down the street in the direction the miners had taken Jasper's body. "You know, Jasper seemed to be a good guy. Can't blame him much for wanting to make a little money. But he had no idea what Duke was up to. I'd like to help bury Jasper before we leave." The two men headed back to the livery and got Oscar out of the sorrel's stall.

Bart and Luke came from behind the sheriff's office,

carrying shovels, leading the mule with Jasper's body. As they headed for the graveyard, Harvey and Brady fell in behind them.

"Do you mind if we come along to help?" Brady asked.

Bart stopped and glanced back at the two men. "Always glad to have extra hands. C'mon along."

The group moved slowly past rundown shacks surrounded by weeds. Some had a shed for a horse or mule. The whole area had a sad, last-chance atmosphere, as if it knew those who lived here were not going to make the big strike, find their fortune. Those who had made it had already moved out of the shacks.

As they approached the cemetery, Brady picked up a short piece of broken board he had noticed on the ground. "This'll make a marker," he mused.

The cemetery resembled the rest of the area. Graves were scattered about in no particular order. Few had any marking on them to identify the deceased. Harvey looked around, then looked at the board Brady was holding and nodded slightly. Jasper deserved better than an unmarked grave, even though he had reported their location to Duke.

Bart stopped at an unused plot and got shovels from the back of the mule. "Who wants to be first?" he asked. Brady and Harvey reached for the shovels while Bart and Luke marked off the area for the grave. They were surprised to find the ground easy to dig. Recent rains would make the job go quickly. They dug. Oscar kept watch.

Brady handed his shovel to Bart, took out his knife and began scratching JASPER WATTS into the wood. When the grave was deep enough, the four men lowered Jasper's body into the hole. They buried Jasper Watts, his tin coffee cup still in his jacket pocket. His boots were still soggy, the hems of his pants still wet. There was no bag of dust or nuggets with him, no identification, no rings or coins. Apparently he left the world with about the same worldly goods as when he came into it.

Brady propped up the marker with stones so the name was visible. It wouldn't stay standing long; it was as temporary as the entire settlement. Brady was satisfied that at least for a little while, Jasper would be remembered by any who came here.

"Thanks, men," Bart said solemnly, and he and Luke headed back to town.

It was late afternoon, and Brady decided to double check supplies before they began trailing Duke and Cora. Harvey said he had some tribal people camped nearby and would go there for the night. There was a good chance his friends would be aware of someone leaving the settlement in a hurry and trying to stay out of sight. "I am back before sun. We go then," he told Brady as he left.

* * *

Brady picked up a few more items at the general store. Cans of peaches, more leather thongs, a bar of soap. A new leather shirt for Harvey--he would now for sure be Harvey Two Shirts.

A dog was sleeping by the owner's chair but woke up enough to wag his tail at Brady. Brady spoke to him, "Hey old fella, how you doing?" and got another wag of the tail in return. That prompted him. "Do you have any extra bones or scraps a dog would like?"

"I keep a little on hand for this old boy," he replied. "You got a dog, huh? He ougta like a bone or two to chew on, maybe some chunks of fat, too." He never stopped talking while he went into the back room and brought back a small package.

"Thanks," Brady said. "He's a good dog; he deserves something extra." Supplies in hand, Brady headed back to the livery stable. After he unrolled his bed in the hay, he got a piece of jerky for himself and gave Oscar a bone and a bit of fat. Oscar lay down with a big sigh of contentment as he chewed on the bone.

He didn't rest well. Horses in the stalls up the aisle stomped and snorted. He heard Zach give his spiel about his shortened name to another cowboy. Somebody trotted a horse along the back side of the livery, causing Oscar to get up and take a look. Worries and memories came in and out of Brady's head. He missed having Harvey help keep a watch. It wasn't a good night.

The sky in the east was getting light when Harvey returned. Brady had his gear cleaned and packed, nearly ready for whenever they might leave. Harvey didn't speak when Brady handed him the new shirt; he held it up high, nodded, then put it in one of his packs. It didn't take long for Harvey to start telling what he had learned.

"Man, woman on horses. Lead mule with big pack. Headed that way." Harvey pointed the direction Brady had figured they would go. "Tried not to meet anybody. Woman not happy. Loud, yell at man. They not know my people watch them."

Brady chuckled. That sounded like Duke and Cora. Thinking they were smart, trying not to be seen or followed but arguing, loud, probably leaving an obvious trail they could follow. He was pretty sure they weren't smart enough to start a different direction, not head straight toward their destination. Duke didn't seem to think beyond what he wanted nor to consider any consequences before he acted. Brady wondered--not for the first time--what the tie was that bound Duke and Cora so closely. They had much in common: greed, lack of ethics, ruthlessness--but each had an unpleasant temperament. Strange that they were so committed to each other.

* * *

Brady went back to the saloon--again to indulge himself in a beer and to learn more about Duke and Cora. It was pretty warm, he was tired already, and the cool, dark saloon seemed inviting. The bartender lifted a hand in greeting, then said, "Sorry, the beer is warm today. Wagon from the ice house hasn't come in yet."

"No problem, long as it's wet." Incredibly, the same miner was there, talking, talking, talking. Brady occasionally asked a question or commented but there was nothing new in what the miner expounded upon. After listening for several minutes Brady changed the subject.

"So what do folks do around here when they're not on their claims?"

"Well, mostly poker, I guess. Once in a while a guy with a fiddle comes along and plays in the saloon. And couple a weeks ago, some fella came in with fightin' chickens. Damnedest thing you ever saw. Feathers and blood ever'where. Guys bettin' like crazy." He turned to the bartender, signaled for another beer. The guy would spend the rest of the day here, apparently. "Ya know, they put some kinda spurs on them chickens. And they're vicious, bloodthirsty critters, for sure."

When Brady finally got up to leave, he had a much better idea of what to expect around the town. He walked to the diner, thinking it would be a good idea to take some food back to the stable for all of them.

As he approached the diner, he saw what looked like a fight up the street a little way. One man was being beaten by three other men. The outnumbered man was returning punches, but he seemed to be getting the worst of the fight. Suddenly Brady realized the man being beaten looked mighty familiar: Harvey was the one under attack! As Brady ran toward the fight, he could see Harvey must have gotten in some good punches before the three overpowered him. They all had bloody faces and heads and moved sluggishly.

Brady ran through the crowd, pushing men out of the way, and grabbed Harvey just as he began to fall.

"What's goin' on here?" he yelled. "Back off!" The others were startled and stepped back. "What happened? What's this all about?" He was helping Harvey steady himself.

"That Injun stole our money," one man yelled. "Get outa the way!"

"No! Get back and tell me what the hell's goin' on! This is my partner. I'll shoot the first man that tries to lay another hand on him." He had the Winchester in his hand, and his voice let it be known it could be put to quick use.

"We had a horse race. Joe here has one of the best horses in the territory. No one will race him anymore. So this Injun says he'll run his horse against Joe's." The man wiped his face with shirt tail, spit, and continued. "He was mighty willing to bet anyone. Well, he led this old rundown, half-starved pony out and said he'd bet anybody." He straightened, maybe stretching a kink out of his back. "Well, if he was dumb enough to make that bet, we'd be fools not to take his money. Lars held all the bets. Ever'body got in."

Brady shook his head in disgust. "Do I have this straight? You saw his old nag and thought you had a sure-fire bet. You made it a mile-long race out across the field, and that old horse ran the legs off Joe's horse?" His look gave them no pity. "You were gonna be happy to cheat this Indian--his name is Harvey--out of his money, and now you're mad because you think HE cheated YOU?" Brady shook his head again. "You were too dumb to figure out if a total stranger offered that kind of bet you better know more about what he had." Brady was yelling by the time he finished talking. Then he took a deep breath and started yelling again.

"Well, you don't get all the money! Lars better be honest or your fight is with him. Give me Harvey's money, you all get your own back, and nobody loses. Don't even think about trying to keep it all! Lars! Give me Harvey's money!"

The crowd was stunned and no one said a word. This sudden turn of events left them silent for a few minutes. Lars handed over Harvey's money before anyone could think about protesting. Brady put his arm around Harvey's waist, picked up Old Horse's reins, and they hobbled back to the stable. Brady grinned to himself. "Sure wish I coulda seen him run."

He spread Harvey's blankets out on the hay and helped him get as comfortable as possible. Brady helped Harvey check himself over and they didn't find anything broken. Harvey's body was badly bruised and cut, but the bleeding from his face and head had stopped. The body bruises were turning deep purple. He would be in pain and find movement difficult for several days.

"You sleep, Harvey. I'll take care of Old Horse. He's earned some extra feed."

Oscar wagged his tail as he was let out of the sorrel's

stall, then lay down beside Harvey. It hurt to move his arm, but Harvey patted the dog's head softly. "Oscar take care of me." The dog stayed close to his friend's side, even as he gnawed on the bone Brady bought for him.

"Harvey, I don't get it;. Why didn't you pull your knife or your gun? And how did you manage to let three of them gang up on you?"

Although it was painful, Harvey shrugged. "Bad day."

* * *

Morning came pretty early for Harvey, but he got painfully to his feet. He walked slowly around the stable for a few minutes, then gradually began to move a little more easily. Brady got out some day-old frybread and jerky for them all, then set about cleaning stalls, brushing the horses. He would spend the rest of the day scouting out neighboring campsites and settlements, letting Harvey rest.

Brady ran into Zach as he prepared to head out. He settled with Zach for the short time they'd been there and thanked him for the extra help they'd been given.

"We'll be stayin' on a couple more days, but not long."

Zach gave him a toothy grin. "It's shore been good havin' you here. And when you come back through, I hope you'll come back by. If I'm not here when you're ready to leave, just leave your cash in the feed bucket in that first stall. Or you can even wait until you come back by. I know you're good for it."

Brady rode out at a good pace and looked over rough sites in each of the main directions from the settlement. He was careful not to get too close to any, figuring there might be a slim chance Duke was still close by. If Harvey hadn't got hurt, they'd have headed out that day. But Harvey's condition wasn't good, and he was too important for Brady to neglect in any way.

In the late afternoon, Brady returned to the settlement, stopped by the little store and got Harvey a can of peaches, a few strips of streaked meat and a potato. And eggs! A dozen eggs. Nothing but the best for the patient.

Harvey was much improved when Brady pulled up to the

livery. He was up and about, brushing Oscar, humming in his strange way.

"You feelin' good, huh?"

Harvey shrugged.

"You good enough to head out tomorrow, or do you need more time?"

"We go."

They left town the next day on the main road to the mine, but watched for smaller trails leading off to the south. One-man claims were scattered all around the mountains, so travel would be fairly easy for a while. Once they got beyond the mines, Duke and Cora would find the going rougher. There would probably be no settlements for several days, and they were unfamiliar with this territory.

Brady knew the Army post, Fort Robinson, was somewhere off to the south, but he was confident the couple would stay far away from there. Word of the murder and their escape may have reached the fort, and they would not run the risk of being detained there. He figured their best plan would be to go more southwest, out toward the prairie between these mountains and Denver. There would be some small towns where Duke and Cora could stock up on supplies if necessary, but Brady was pretty sure they wouldn't stay long. It would be important for them to get to a more populated place to disappear.

"Here." Harvey stopped abruptly and looked intently at the ground. A slightly worn trail led off into the trees and up a long hill. Brady looked closely, also. It was obvious horses had turned off here. The dirt was chewed up by hooves, and some small branches broken off where something had rubbed against the bushes and trees. As they looked more closely at the tracks, they could see that one horse or a mule was not staying on the trail. Tracks could be seen in the brush on both sides of the trail, and some of the hoofprints faced sideways, almost backwards. "What do you bet they bought or stole some fresh animals and didn't know what they were getting. Looks like one of them is having trouble with their horse," Brady said. "Sure hope that pony can buck hard." Harvey nodded. Anything that caused trouble for the pair they were following would be an advantage for the trackers.

They followed the trail all afternoon without much trouble. Occasional patches of torn-up grass and brush reinforced their notion that one of the pair was having a lot of trouble with a horse. The terrain was rough in places, with deep draws and steep banks. Late in the afternoon they crested a hill and spotted a prospector working on the bank of a deep gully. He turned toward them as they approached. Brady noticed he kept his hand close to his gun. A quick glance sideways confirmed Harvey's hand was close to his, also. "Howdy," Brady said. "We're just passing by. Looks like you have a lot of work going on here. Hope you're doing okay with it." He tipped his hat. "Name's Brady Quillan. This is Harvey Two Shirts. We're on the trail of a pair. Man and a woman. Wonder if you might have seen them. Have a pack mule with 'em."

The old prospector relaxed a little and leaned on his pick. "Howdy. Name's Harold Moss." He pushed his worn hat back on his head. "Yeah, pair came by late yesterday. Didn't trust the look of 'em a'tall. If I didn't have my shotgun in my hand when they rode up, I'd prob'ly be dead by now. Those folks didn't come up slow and quiet and respectful like you. Made me suspicious right off." He paused for a moment, looked at Brady thoughtfully and said, "What did they do?"

Brady took a deep breath before he answered. "They killed my wife." They all sat for a long moment in silence.

"Mighty sorry," Harold said. "I knew there was something bad about them."

"Did they say anything or give you any idea of where they might be headed or what they had in mind?"

"Naw, not much. I think they would have liked to take whatever I have, but this old gun and the shotgun sort of discouraged them. The lady maybe said something about it bein' time to head for the big city, but I don't know. They left, and I holed up until this morning. Got a good camp that nobody can sneak up on, so they couldn't come back and finish me off at night." He shuffled a ways to his fire pit. "Why don't you fellas camp here tonight? It'll be dark soon. There ain't no water for quite a spell after you leave here. You can water your horses at that spring right over there. I'd be right pleased to have somebody to talk to. Not many folks come by this way."

Brady and Harvey exchanged a glance, then nodded and dismounted. Harold was busy petting Oscar, telling him what a good fella he was. Oscar's tail told how much he was enjoying the attention of the old prospector.

The horses were fed and watered, Oscar watered, bedrolls thrown to the ground. The old prospector shuffled around his fire, poking and stirring. Harvey moved close with his pans and frybread fixin's. Old Moss dabbed lard into a pan and watched it melt, then added oatmeal and coarse cornmeal. The smell wasn't bad, but Brady was already thinking about how dry it was going to be. He motioned to Harvey to start the coffee. On a notion of generosity, Brady offered strips of streaked meat. The aroma got even better, and the three men and Oscar prepared to enjoy the meal. They sat on the ground with their plates, eager to eat and rest.

The sky darkened. They were sipping the last of their coffee when Harvey straightened up suddenly, alert. He pointed toward the trail, and Brady could see the dim outline of two riders a short distance away. Brady alerted the old prospector, motioned for him to stay put and continue with his coffee. Harvey moved to the far side of his horse. Brady double-checked to be sure his Winchester was close by and was pleased to notice that Moss cautiously checked his six-gun and shotgun as well.

In just a few short minutes, the riders were at the edge of the campsite.

"Howdy," one spoke gruffly. "Any water around here?"

Brady nodded. "Yeah, there's a little."

"Well, don't let that old injun use it up on the worthless nag of his," growled the other man.

Brady knew there was going to be trouble. "Sorry, fellas. But as soon as you get a canteen full of water, you can be heading on. This is a permanent campsite, not available for anybody else."

"Nah." The rider hacked out a cough. "My horse is used up. Think I'll just take one of yours. You three get outa here and take that old nag with ya."

The older of the two looked down at Brady as he spoke. His hand lowered to his gun handle and he gave a small, hard sneer. He paid no attention to Harvey Two Shirts, apparently considering him no threat. Brady's cold stare surprised the outlaws, who had expected no resistance. They stared silently at each other for a moment, then the older man began to pull his gun out. Before the gun cleared the holster, a loud gunshot exploded the silence. The outlaw fell to the ground. The second man looked down at his dead companion and started to reach for his own gun.

"Don't even think about it," Brady cautioned.

The outlaw hesitated for a moment, then drew his gun. Brady's hand was faster--and so was Moss. Two gunshots, and the second outlaw fell from his horse.

Brady turned to Harvey and Moss. "Thanks, men. We were close to being in a heap of trouble."

Moss had risen from his place on the ground. "Glad you two were here. Never had much trouble before, but it gets worse all the time, I reckon."

The outlaws' horses stood close by, not spooked by the gunshots. Brady and Harvey lifted the bodies to the saddles, flopped them over, and secured them with their own lariats. Brady told Harvey and Moss his plan--hoping they would agree without argument. He'd lead the horses down the trail toward the town just a couple of miles, then turn the horses loose. They'd head for other horses, feed, water, rest. And Brady, Harvey, and Moss wouldn't have the burden of burial. The men deserved no better, in Brady's mind. And who knows, maybe they had acquaintances who'd take care of the final details. Harvey and Moss gave no argument, and Brady headed off down the trail. He didn't like the idea of responsibility for the end of more lives; but he didn't like the idea of being the victim of criminal intent, either. No doubt Harvey would have a philosophical observation of the whole event.

* * *

Brady returned to the campsite, satisfied with his actions. What's done was done; it was time to think more about where they were going and what they needed to do. He wished they had found out more about Duke and Cora in the settlement. Many seemed to know who they were, but no one knew anything specific about them except they were unfriendly, aggressive, loud, and kept to themselves.

Brady and Harvey decided it made sense to stay one more night with Moss. It would be better to be nowhere around when the horses were found.

Brady spent a restless night. He was sorry gunfire had been necessary, but he was realistic. The outlaws would not have left them alive; they had had to protect themselves.

The question of where they would go filled Brady's mind for hours. How could they figure out which direction the pair might have taken? After hours of tossing, turning, and rejecting his own ideas, Brady had one idea that seemed like it might have possibilities. Duke and Cora had lived in a shack by themselves all the time they were at the settlement. They were probably looking for money, a chance to get rich. Maybe he could find something in that shack that would be a clue to where they headed. Brady was sure they had a destination in mind; they had a plan and were not just running. They had left in a hurry; there might be a small bit of evidence left behind.

Brady was pretty sure no one would have gone near the shack in case the unpredictable pair came back. The more he thought about it, the more likely it seemed there might be some kind of clue in the shack. He made up his mind: they would go back to the settlement before continuing on.

Chapter 14

Friendships weren't really made in a mining settlement. Every relationship seemed tentative. Nevertheless, Brady was a bit reluctant to leave Moss. Moss seemed to be a generous, trusting man, and there were few like him. But they needed to leave promptly. A quick breakfast and a second cup of coffee while they talked over their close call, and Brady, Harvey, and Oscar took their leave.

The trio moved back down to the settlement, and Brady was again struck by the mixture of people there. Old and young white men, a few Indians; Orientals who seemed to stick together, a couple of saloon girls in worn satin dresses. Shopkeepers looking frazzled and worn out. In fact, nearly everybody looked worn out. There were very few children-- more stray dogs than kids.

The settlement was more lawless than Brady had expected. He began to wonder if any word of Duke's involvement in Sullie's death had even reached the law officers here. And he wondered about their own gunplay that resulted in deaths. Even though they were in self-defense, it would seem the law might be expected to do some investigation.

They settled into a rough camp just a way up the mountain. Several other campfires were already lit, and it seemed noisy to Brady--horses stomping, men talking, swearing, laughing; dogs barking. Oscar was quiet--probably too tired to worry about it.

Harvey did his magic with the wajapi, and Brady surprised him with a couple strips of buffalo he had bought at the general store. It was a great meal--the aroma while it cooked was almost more than Brady could stand. He was tempted to spear a strip of buffalo before Harvey signaled it was ready.

They had settled on a log to eat the rare feast when they were aware of a rider leading a mule, coming down the mountain path. A good-sized burden was on the mule, and Brady cringed at the notion that it was another body. This many people, this much trouble--this was a place he didn't want to hang around. Harvey, too, looked at the rider with the pack animal, then put his plate aside and stood, gun in hand.

Brady stood as well and moved closer to the trail. He hailed the rider, although he was reluctant to have any part of this scene, even to inquire about the mule's burden. "Looks like another death. Hope it was illness, not anything else."

The old rider reined up, shook his head and grunted. "Nope. Guy got shot."

"How'd it happen?"

"Ain't figured that out totally yet. Somebody thought he was bein' too nosy around a campsite and took at shot at him. Didn't miss."

"Was he a friend of yours? Did you know who shot him? Or whose campsite it was?"

"Nope. I knew him a little. Drank a little whiskey with him a few times. He was panning a little creek close to where I was. Neither one of us did much good." The old man shook his head, winced. "I guess I got to bury him. Ain't nobody else around who knew him a'tall."

Brady didn't hesitate before he spoke. "We'll help you. Where you gonna bury him?"

Harvey was startled. But only briefly. He moved closer to Brady, nodding agreement.

"Yonder by that little church is okay. They have other miners there, and they have room. Appreciate your offer. I'm stiff. Can use the help."

The church was close by, the ground not too hard, and the work went quickly. The old man had pick and shovel, and the three of them were able to dig a decent grave for the corpse.

"What's the guy's name? Seems strange to be digging a grave for somebody I don't know."

"I only know Morton. Don't know if that's last name or first name. Sorta pitiful, ain't it?"

As they worked, Brady tried to pry more information from the old man. It was mostly a futile effort, but he did learn that the shooter was a young man--a boy, really--hired to keep an eye on a campsite belonging to somebody who was going to be away for just a couple of hours. The old man opined that

Morton may have just been rifling through some gear looking for vittles or coffee when he was seen and shot. He didn't know the name of the shooter or the man who hired him. It was, as the old man observed, pitiful. The grave was unmarked. Bleak. But at least he hadn't been left for the buzzards or coyotes.

Brady and Harvey headed back to the livery. Brady had an itch to know the name of the kid who shot Morton and the name of the guy who hired him. Maybe there was no connection to anything Brady and Harvey were concerned with, but Brady knew to follow up on hunches. They each went back to their best sources of information: Harvey to the front of the saloon, Brady to the general store and later back to the livery.

It was only a couple of hours before Harvey returned with the information that the kid who shot Morton lived at the western edge of the settlement on a small spread with his mother and several brothers and sisters. Brady headed for his saddle almost before Harvey finished the telling.

"Know the kid's name?"

Harvey shook his head.

It took a short while to reach the edge of the settlement. They passed three small shacks with fenced corrals, then came upon one that looked as if several people might be crammed in. A rocking chair, a couple of stools, and several wooden boxes were on the rickety porch. An assortment of ragged clothing hung on a wire stretched between two poles supporting a sagging porch roof.

They pulled up at the edge of what might be considered a yard. Brady dismounted and handed his reins to Harvey. As he started for the porch, the screened door opened and a small boy stepped out.

"Hold it, mister. You got business here?" The boy's voice was belligerent, his jaw stuck out assertively. He was barefooted, his britches held up with a belt a foot too large for him, the extra length hanging down past his knees. He looked to be about six or seven years old. Skinny. Tanned and not real clean.

"Sorry. We don't mean to intrude. Just wanted to get some directions." Brady was easing a little closer to the boy, step by step.

"D'rections to where?"

"Lookin' for a camp where some miners stay." Close enough now to see the holes in the boy's shirt.

"Ain't none right around here. Better go back to town."

"You by yourself here?" Brady was within ten feet of the boy. Suddenly the screened door snapped opened and a woman stepped out.

"Mister, you got no business here. Move on out."

"Sorry, ma'am. Just tellin' the boy here we're looking for a camp where some people we're lookin' for might have stayed."

"Nobody stayed around here. You go on now." She looked tired and worn, like most of the few women in the settlement. It was no easy place for any female.

"Ma'am, could I just talk to you for a minute or two? I think you can maybe help me with a real bad problem." Brady tried his best to sound sincere. Decent. Harmless. Sincere.

"I don't think I can help you with anything. Go on back to town."

"Ma'am. It's about the shooting." It was a risk, Brady knew, but maybe it would work. "The shooting your boy was involved with."

The woman inhaled quickly, stepped back, and reached for the boy's hand.

"I can't help you with that. You've got the wrong place." Her voice was weak, unconvincing.

"But we might be able to help YOU, ma'am. We're trying to settle some things, and your boy can maybe help us. We're not here to hurt him in any way." Brady had continued his movement toward the porch and was now right in front of the woman and her boy. He held his hat in his hands, tried to look the woman straight in the eye. "I think maybe your boy was hired by a man who was on the wrong side of the law, and your boy just got caught up in something he couldn't have known about ahead of time." It was an exaggeration of a hunch, sure; but maybe it was a valid one. Maybe there was something here related to Duke Marsh. It seemed like a good possibility Duke would have hired a half-spooked kid to guard his campsite, maybe even considering the possibility that a gunshot might occur. Probably didn't figure it would involve a death, but a nervous kid could scare off a snoopy, sticky-fingered intruder. And for a few coins, a buck or two, he could leave his campsite for a short while, take care of who knows what kind of business.

The woman seemed to be wavering. Brady didn't push it, just bided his time. Finally, the woman took a deep breath and nodded. "Have a seat here on the porch. We'll talk for just a few minutes. See what your problem is."

Brady sat on the porch step; the woman moved to the rocking chair. The boy stood holding on to one of the porch posts, watching Brady's every move, glancing occasionally at Harvey, who stayed at a distance with the horses.

Brady told the woman quickly and with little detail that he was trailing a man and a woman who were killers and thieves, and that they may be in the area. He planned to have them arrested and taken back to their home area for trial. There were warrants out for their arrest, and he was closely tied to the victims of their criminal acts.

The woman listened carefully, nodding a couple of times, then said quietly, "My son is young, but he tries hard to be an adult. His father is up at the mines and probably won't be back for quite a while. We're trying to make it here without him. My son--Richard is his name--spends a lot of time in the settlement and up where the miners hang out." She stopped for a minute, then continued. "He picks up odd jobs once in a while, and this one was gonna be a good one. All he had to do was sit at the campsite and be sure nobody got into the stuff that was piled up there. He was told to shoot at anybody who showed up." Her voice broke then, quavered as she continued. "Somebody did come and was goin' through the gear. Richard shot. He had no idea he'd hit the guy." She had to stop again to get control. "Richard is hiding out until all this quiets down."

"Ma'am, I'm so sorry. This is rough on your whole family. Can you tell me where he is so I can talk to him? I need to know who hired him."

"I don't think he even knows the guy's name. It was a man and his wife. And maybe they had good luck at the mines or something, because Richard said they had plenty of money. The guy told Richard to get the hell out of the camp site and not come back. He took his rifle back and paid him twice what he had promised." She wiped her eyes with her shirt tail. "That's all I can tell you."

"Can you tell me where the camp site is?"

"Only that it's about halfway up the mountain and that there's a creek running beside it. And there's room to picket a couple of horses."

Brady hated to leave this woman, thinking there may still be a bit of information that might come out. But he had much more than he'd thought he'd get--and more clues to finding Duke and Cora. Soon. "Thank you so much, ma'am. You've been a big help. Good luck to you." He took a few folded bills from his pocket, pressed them into the woman's hand, nodded to the kid and stepped toward his horse. Harvey was mounted, ready to ride, and they headed back toward the settlement. The hunch had paid off, for sure.

They had not gone far when Harvey pulled up and looked back toward the little house they had just left. The kid was running hard, trying to catch up to them. Brady reined the sorrel to face the kid.

"Wait, mister. Just please wait." The boy hurried up to them, panting. "Please just listen to me a minute."

Brady wrinkled his brow a bit. "What's on your mind?"

"You gave my ma money. That's a big help for us." He scuffled his bare feet in the dust, then continued. "I was thinking maybe you could help Richard."

"Son, we can't help Richard. We don't know anybody around here, and we don't really know everything that happened with Richard and the guy he shot."

"But mister..." The boy's voice cracked a bit. "Maybe you could just help us think what to do next."

Brady sat back in his saddle. "Maybe your brother should trust the sheriff. If he didn't really mean to shoot the man, if it was an accident, maybe the sheriff can help him."

"Richard's afraid of the sheriff, afraid he would take sides with the rich guy."

"I don't know the sheriff, but maybe he's a fair man. We can go by and talk to him, sorta feel him out, see if he has his mind set one way or another about your brother." Brady looked down at the boy, feeling frustration as he wanted to get on with his own investigation but also feeling sympathy for the kid. "But how can we get in touch with you when we find out anything? We can't ride all the way out here again; we gotta get on the trail."

The boy gulped, then took a big breath, his mind made up. "Richard's hidin' out close in town. You could find him there and let him know." He shoved his hands into his pockets, looked up with desperation.

Brady shook his head, blew out a deep breath, looked at Harvey. Harvey was refusing to show an opinion. No nod of any kind. No firming of his jaw. No looking off into the distance.

Brady looked again at the kid. "Okay, kid. Tell us where he is and we'll let him know how the sheriff seems." He thought for just a moment. "We'll go see Richard first, then maybe go to the sheriff, depending on what we learn from Richard."

"Okay, mister. Thanks. You'll see that my brother is a good person." The kid wiped his nose on his forearm, then said quietly, looking behind him as if there might be someone listening. "He's stayin' in a shed behind the store. That little store where the guy has the old dog. That guy knows my dad."

Brady was astounded. In as big a settlement as this was, it seemed risky to be hiding behind a store that would be doing a lot of business. And surprised that he himself would have had a connection already to the guy who ran the store--and Brady had a good opinion of him: Kind to animals, kind to humans, apparently.

"You get on back to your mom. Help her as much as you can, and we'll help your brother as much as we can." The kid backed a few steps, then turned and jogged back toward his home.

Harvey finally made a movement. Nodded and said "Washteh. Good." Whether the 'good' was about the kid, Brady's decision to try to help, or the general state of affairs, Brady had no idea. He just nudged the sorrel into a lope and headed for the settlement, Harvey close beside.

Chapter 15

Too many things had kept Brady and Harvey from their main purpose. Now Brady was concerned about the barefoot kid and his trouble-burdened brother. At least Richard had a supportive family and the help of the store owner. Brady figured they could stop by the store and speak to the owner, see the kid's brother, maybe get some help for him. If they could just do it efficiently, without spending much time or getting involved in a lengthy confrontation with anybody, maybe they could be of help. The poor kid--that was a bleak homestead, and even though the kid seemed brave and full of good intentions, he didn't stand much of a chance for a good future. The woman had more than she could handle and she seemed too worn out, too tired. Brady couldn't help but think of the feisty little woman with the shovel. The Ballard woman. She could probably make it out here. Or anywhere.

They rode back into the main road of the settlement and approached the store. Their horses tied to the hitching post, Harvey and Brady entered the store. They were greeted immediately by the owner, and Brady moved close to him so they could speak quietly. There were no other customers in the store, as far as Brady could tell, but he sure didn't want to jeopardize Richard's protection. He had to sidestep the old dog in order to speak softly.

"Wonder if I could speak to you just a bit about your boarder...?"

"Boarder? I don't have any boarders." The store owner wasn't as talkative as when Brady had been in before.

"Yeah. The young man. Richard." Brady looked him directly in the eye.

"Um. Well, supposing I know who you're talking about, what do you need?" The man wiped his hands on his apron, nervous.

"We just came from his home place, and his kid brother told us where to find him. We just need to see if there's anything we can do to help."

"Oh. Well. The young man is well and safe right now. Far as I know, you're the only ones lookin' for him. But he's scared." The man looked toward the door, looked around the store again, then looked at Brady.

Brady continued. "Any chance he won't get arrested if he comes out?"

"I don't think the sheriff is lookin' for him. All the sheriff knows is that a guy got killed. There's so much shootin' around here, I don't think the sheriff has a prayer of followin' up on much of it. But just for the record, I think he's a pretty straight fella. Mostly just overworked."

"This Richard has to feel safe enough to get back to his home and to be able to work a little, like he did before."

"I don't think it'd be a good idea for him to go back up to the camps right now. That guy he was working for is a pretty rough fella, I think. Richard doesn't need to run into him again any time soon. But about the shooting...do you think that might eventually be a more serious thing?"

"I don't think the guy--Morton was his name--had any connections much around here. And the guy who hired Richard is maybe already outa town. If Richard is careful, he might be able to get on back home and just take his time about lookin' for more work at the camp sites. Whaddya think?"

The man blew out a puff of air. "The boy is a nice young man. I'll help him any way I can. And his dad will be around the camps quite a bit and he'll hear what's goin' on. Mebbe you're right."

"Let's go out to your shed and talk to him. See how he feels about that. Does he have a horse here?"

"Yeah, his horse is in that little pen right by the shed. And I'll go with you so he knows it's safe to open the door."

They moved out to the shed. Brady noticed the horse--more of a pony, really--was small but looked healthy enough. There had probably been more to eat here than back at the home place. And that might have been the case for Richard, as well.

The door was opened. "Richard, don't worry. These guys

are safe," the store owner said, then went back inside his place, and Harvey and Brady squeezed into the shed. It was as dark inside as an outhouse, the only light coming from the half-open door. Richard was small, dirty, tense. His eyes were wide, and he gulped and fidgeted, then asked, "Who are you? Whaddya want?"

Brady tried to put him at ease. He repeated the discussion they'd had with the store owner, asked Richard many questions about what had happened, what he had done since the shooting--as much information as he could get from the nervous boy.

"Your little brother asked us to come here, to help if we could. I don't think we can do much for you, but I think you can do a lot for yourself. What you did was an accident. You're lucky that the situation here as far as law enforcement is so overwhelmed with work you prob'ly won't get much attention. Remember: It was an accident." Brady's voice was calm and quiet. "Just how old are you?"

"Fifteen."

Brady looked at him sternly.

"My next birthday."

Brady looked solemnly at the young man. "I think if I was you, I'd go to the sheriff first thing and let him know what happened. You can let him know the man you shot is buried, that you're not even sure how the shooting happened. Be honest with him. I think you'll see he doesn't want to take any time lookin' into things."

It was true. This IS what Brady would do. He looked at Harvey and felt Harvey's agreement. Harvey and Brady had both been involved in killings recently; it didn't take much of a stretch to make their situation as dire as Richard considered his own. Brady wasn't going to go admit any killing, however. He had justified their actions as self-defense. Richard could work on his own justification. Brady and Harvey would be leaving the settlement very soon; it would be Richard's town for as long as his family stayed. It had to be safe for him--as safe as the lawless place could be.

Richard seemed a little less tense by the time they finished their talk. The young man's voice was steady as he spoke. "Thank you both. I panicked, for sure. I never been in a thing like this before. But I think you're right. I'll see the sheriff as soon as I see he's in his office. I can find work around home until my dad gets back. Or maybe I can find him up at the camps. But anyway, thank you a whole lot."

Brady reached in his pocket and pulled out a couple of bills. "Get a few supplies and head on back to your mom as soon as you can. She'll be needin' you. You have a fine family. Help 'em as much as you can." Brady offered his hand, and Richard didn't hesitate to shake it....and didn't hesitate to offer his hand to Harvey. Harvey hadn't said a word, but Richard obviously understood he was in total agreement with all that had been said.

They went back into the store, told the owner what had transpired, and headed out to their horses. Harvey's only comment about the whole situation was, "Small horse."

Chapter 16

Brady was resting at the livery, trying to ease his mind about how things might be back at the ranch, how Tassle might be faring with chores, livestock, and concerns about Dutch Heisler; worries about how to shorten the distance to Duke and Cora, and the deep grief he felt about Sullie. He also had worries about the law--just how much trouble might he and Harvey Two Shirts face with the killing of the outlaws and the crippling of the would-be thief, about young Richard. And damn, they had to start worrying about the weather. It'd be cold and snowy soon; they'd need extra gear and clothing. Harvey had gone back to his post at the diner to see what more he could learn about Duke--his whereabouts and his legal situation; Brady would meet him later to compare notes. It was for sure they couldn't waste time and horseflesh on a dead-end trail. They had to be sure which way Duke and Cora were headed.

There seemed to be more chatter coming from the saloon, more bustling around, more shouting. It was always a busy place, but this afternoon seemed busier than usual. He tipped his hat up and focused more intently on the entrance. A few miners and cowboys seemed to be arguing in a fairly friendly manner with only occasional angry outbursts, and he could see money changing hands. It was more than just an ante-up for poker.

Harvey appeared suddenly, Oscar tagging along behind. "Horse race tomorrow," he said. "Big."

"Where in the world would they run a race around here?" There were no areas like fairgrounds or ball fields anywhere close, as far as Brady could tell.

"This road. In town. Here."

That was hard for Brady to imagine. The road was narrow, mostly clogged with hitched mules and horses, a few wagons and abandoned gear, stray dogs. Harvey's race with Old Horse across the field was one thing. A race the whole settlement was interested in was something entirely different. "Maybe we should check around for some more details. Find out exactly the starting point, see who's entering horses. See if we can check out the horses ourselves before tomorrow. Find out what time the race starts."

Harvey nodded, stepped aside and waited for Brady to stand up. They put Oscar in the stall with the sorrel and headed for the saloon. Harvey walked slightly behind, leaving Brady to lead the way to the gathering. Brady nodded to a large cowboy and asked, "What's this about a race?"

The cowboy pushed his hat back on his head and said, "Yeah. It'll be tomorrow morning. Right here in town. Pretty high stakes, if the betting keeps up."

The miners and cowboys seemed to be jostling around and Brady was concerned about the possibility it might get a little rough. He thought then about the chatty cook at the diner. He and Harvey left the rowdy crowd and headed up the street. Harvey took his regular seat on the bench in front and Brady entered.

"Well, hello! You're the guy who feeds his dog beef sandwiches, right?" the cook greeted, wiping his hands on his grimy apron.

"Yeah. Good to see you. Could you fix me a couple of those beef sandwiches? Well, make it three."

"Sure thing."

"What's the deal on this horse race I hear about?"

The cook started slicing bread, arranging sliced meat and pickles. "Yeah. Sorta a weird deal. Started in a poker game last night. Pretty high stakes. Guy ran outa cash, put up his horse. Claimed he was real fast, could run the feet off anything around here." He slapped several slices of beef on the bread, forked a few sliced pickles on it, mashed another slice of bread on top. "Guy didn't really think he'd lose his horse, but he did. And then the guy who won the pot started yellin' about how the horse might not be worth the two hundred bucks he was in for. Came close to a fist fight, but the bartender sorta stepped in and they finally agreed there'd be a race to see if the horse was as good as the guy said." He put two more sandwiches together in double time.

"You can leave the pickles offa one of those," Brady directed. "How does the betting go? Who holds the bets, decides the odds?"

"That'd be the deputy. Only one anybody'd trust. Pot will be big. Four horses in. Another guy offered to run two of his to make it a bigger race and the banker has a kinda fancy horse he thinks can run some."

The cook wrapped the sandwiches in brown paper, palmed the coins Brady held out. "To tell the truth of it, I think prob'ly the poker horse can win it, but you never know."

"Well, thanks. It'll be interesting to see how they can clear this road enough to have room for four horses to run."

"Oh, they can do that. Ran a chuckwagon race here coupla weeks ago. Right down the road. Turned, and raced back. Only one wagon wrecked. Driver hurt pretty bad but it was a good race."

"Reckon that's how this race will go? Down the road, turn, and come back? "

"Yep. Start just past the livery, go half a mile, turn, and come back. Dirt'll fly."

"Sounds like somethin' to see. Thanks for the sandwiches. And the information. Be seein' ya."

"Yep. Stop in again soon."

Harvey and Oscar were glad to see the beef sandwiches, and Brady told Harvey how the race would be run. Harvey seemed real interested. As soon as his sandwich was finished, he moved toward the road.

"You lookin' for the horses?"

Harvey nodded.

"Believe I'll just stay right here and think about it for a while. Oscar can stay with me." Brady figured Harvey would take a while looking at the four horses.... if he could even find them. And Brady still needed to work on clearing his mind. Also, he didn't want to spend much time in crowds. He sure didn't want Duke to catch sight of him, if Duke was even around. Harvey would be safe out and about. But Duke would recognize Brady and Oscar. Best to stay put. He'd feed horses, tidy up the gear, ease his mind.

* * *

Harvey returned a couple of hours later. He sat, rubbed Oscar's ears, grunted a couple of times.

"Find the horses?"

Harvey nodded.

"They look any quick?"

Harvey nodded.

"Any one in particular?"

Harvey nodded.

"Worth putting a bet on?"

Harvey shrugged.

"We'll have a good place to watch from, right here."

Harvey nodded.

"Want me to make a wager for you?"

Harvey shrugged.

"Maybe wait 'til tomorrow?"

Harvey nodded.

Morning found Harvey behind the livery, making coffee and wajapi. Brady wouldn't have minded a little streaked meat to go with it, but that apparently wasn't on the morning menu. Harvey ate quickly, then cleaned the cooking things and nodded toward the front entrance.

"You goin' to look at the horses again? Want me to go with you?"

Harvey nodded, then shrugged.

There weren't many folks in the street yet, and though some of the rigs had been moved during the night, the street was still cluttered. It seemed strange to Brady that none of the race horses were stabled at the livery. Must belong to folks who had a little pasture area or a barn. No doubt Harvey had staked it all out.

They left Oscar with the sorrel and headed out toward the west. Harvey seemed to know where he was going, and Brady was glad to leave it in his hands. In a short distnce, they came to a little barn with two horses in a small paddock. Harvey squinted at them, grunted, moved to the fence. Brady looked closely. The horses looked like nothing to brag about, but at least they were clean and looked fit. Harvey studied them for a while longer, then moved away. Brady followed.

In just a few yards, they came to a small tent with a fire pit beside it, a horse picketed at the rear. Harvey moved closer but kept a respectable distance from the tent flap. The horse was nice looking, wide in the rear end and broad in the chest. He snorted a little, looked at them with interest. The tent flap moved and a cowboy emerged.

"Whaddya want here, boys?" The cowboy slapped a hat against his thigh, combed his hair with his fingers, and put the hat on.

Brady nodded, touched the brim of his hat, and stepped forward a bit. "Just interested in your horse here."

"Yeah. Well, we don't need much company. It's a big day for him and I don't want any commotion."

"Don't want to bother. Not from around here. Just trying to figure out this race thing."

"Mister, NOBODY's from around here. You best be movin' on. Maybe see you at the race this morning."

"Yeah. Well, good luck to ya. Nice lookin' horse." Brady and Harvey backed up a step or two, then turned to leave.

"Don't mean to be inhospitable. Just bein' careful. Don't trust some of these folks around here." The cowboy sounded sincere, a little regretful.

"Don't blame ya. We'll be watchin the race. Stay safe."

"Thanks. We'll try."

Brady and Harvey moved back toward the road and Harvey headed on farther west. Fairly close, they came to a real house---wood, with windows and a fenced yard. At the back was a taller fence with a small run-in and a water tank. A shiny bay paced along the fence, his nose lifted, sniffing out the company. He was long and tall, very clean. This must be the banker's horse.

Harvey didn't waste much time looking at him. Brady admired the horse but figured the cowboy's horse looked a little more likely to be quick. This horse might go a longer distance, but maybe the cowboy's horse was tougher. He wondered what Harvey thought. It would come out eventually.

They headed back toward the main part of the little town, back to the livery. Oscar was glad to see them, glad to see his water bowl filled. They checked the horses' water and hay, shoveled out the manure. No words spoken yet.

Finally, the few chores done, they sat in the shade. There was a bit of coffee left in the pot, and they each had a slug of the cold, strong stuff.

"Well, Harvey. What do you think about the race?"

"Cowboy should win. But there will be trouble."

"What kind of trouble?"

"Much money, much trouble."

"You think somebody will try to throw the race?"

Harvey nodded.

"How do you think they'd do it?"

Harvey waited a moment, then said firmly. "Hurt horse. Hurt rider."

"Surely they'll be watching for that. Especially with a lot of money on the race."

Harvey nodded again.

"Maybe we should help keep a watch on things, ya think?"

Harvey shook his head no. "I watch horses. You watch for Duke."

"The horses are too far apart for you to watch all four. I can keep low, maybe watch from a distance."

Brady had good thoughts about the cowboy and sure didn't want either the cowboy or his horse hurt. He knew it was this horse that was the poker horse. If the money was on him to win and he got hurt and another horse won, the pot would be sizable. But they needed to check how the betting was going, what the odds were. Where was the deputy headquartered? Bets taken in the sheriff's office? Now that should be a long shot. But this was, after all, a mining community, where anything goes.

* * *

The early morning chill eased, and things started getting livelier in the street. Buggies and wagons were moved, trash and gear mostly cleared away. A couple of old men had moved chairs closer to the road, and store owners were clearing their doorways, maybe for shoppers to come in but more likely for the owners to have a clear view of the "track". Just west of the livery, there was activity of a different sort. The four horses were there, getting tacked up. The big bay wore a racing saddle; the other three had western gear. A skinny little guy would apparently be the rider on the bay; the cowboy looked to be his own jockey, and the other two horses had young boys standing close by, ready to mount up. The bay seemed nervous; the other three horses just looked interested in the commotion.

The deputy had moved from the sheriff's office down the street toward the starting point. Miners and cowboys still approached him to bet. The deputy held a fistful of paper money and held a box for coins. He carried a notebook and wrote names, choices, and amounts.

Harvey signaled that he would be on his own for a while and moved like a shadow among the crowd. He edged around the two horses and their owner and the two young riders, then moved closer to the big bay. He slipped easily among the bystanders, attracting no attention. Then he was close to the cowboy and the poker horse. He moved quietly to the edge of the bystanders, then stood, unmoving, watching the crowd and the horses. He could see all four horses from his vantage point, and he was aware of each person in the vicinity.

"Riders, prepare to mount. The race will begin in ten minutes." The loud voice boomed through a megaphone.

Harvey moved quietly toward the side of the cowboy with the poker horse. He touched the man's arm, then said softly, "Check your cinch." The cowboy looked startled, mildly agitated, but then lifted the fender on the left, lowered it, then lifted the fender on the right and gasped. The girth had been sliced nearly completely through, was held together by just a few strands. "Damn! What in hell?!?" He unbuckled the damaged girth and held it up. The man with the two entries looked toward him. "Whoa, that's bad luck, friend. I have an extra if you need it."

"I shore do. Thanks. Can't imagine how this happened. Fairly new cinch." The man shuffled to a gear bag, lifted a cinch and handed it to the cowboy. "We'll settle later, if that's okay," said the cowboy, and moved to attach the borrowed cinch to his saddle.

"Man," he said to Harvey, "that would have been a disaster. How'd you know that?" Harvey only shrugged, then said quietly, "Don't drink from you canteen." The cowboy's canteen hung on a post close to the saddling area. He looked at Harvey with a question on his face. Harvey shrugged; the cowboy nodded.

"Five minutes," bellowed the man with the megaphone. Harvey moved quickly back past the livery, then on along the road toward the half-mile turning point. There wouldn't be much he could do to prevent sabotage of racing horses, but he could at least holler to warn of trouble if he saw anything suspicious. He was quite sure the cowboy would listen to him, even if nobody else did.

Brady stood just at the front of the livery, a good place to watch the start of the race. Although he was not a gambling man, he had placed a wager: The poker horse looked good to him, and the cowboy seemed a decent sort. He watched Harvey moving quickly but silently along the road toward the turning point. He didn't know what Harvey had in mind, but he knew his friend would keep a close eye on the race.

The four horses were lined up at the foot of the street, three standing fairly quietly, the bay dancing. The megaphone blared again. "The race will begin at the end of a count of three with a pistol shot. Horses will run half a mile, turn, and the race will end here, where it began. The judge's call will be final. No more bets taken at this time. May the best horse win."

The crowd had spread out, evenly spaced along the first portion of the race. Brady couldn't see clear to the end, but there were spectators far out as well.

"Your attention, please! THREE! TWO! ONE!" The sharp pop of a pistol! The bay jumped wildly but soon settled back, the jockey nearly unseated but quickly back in control. The other three horses seemed only mildly startled and moved out at a gallop. The cowboy seemed confident, his horse looking alert and mindful not of the unruly crowd but of his rider. The two ranch horses settled behind the bay and the poker horse, moving at a good pace. In a few seconds, Brady moved slightly toward the center of the road to get a better look at the four critters almost neck and neck now. the bay moving with a long stride, the ranch horses almost at a dead run. The poker horse moved quickly but evenly; the cowboy leaned slightly forward, not spurring but evidently using only his voice to move the poker horse along.

Harvey was only about three quarters of the way to the turning point when he saw two men slightly ahead of him, on the other side of the road. One held a long stick, the other a scarf. He didn't know their plan, but the stuff they held didn't belong to the event. He ran quickly to the other side, just a few seconds ahead of the racing horses. The two men looked at him briefly with scorn, then turned their attention back to the race. Harvey moved closer to the men, watching closely. As the horses approached, it became apparent the man with the stick was getting ready to move. He lifted the stick, started to move closer to the track. Harvey lurched quickly from the side, threw the man off balance. The stick fell uselessly to the ground; the man fell as well, unable to regain his balance. Harvey pretended to have lost his balance even more, leaned into the other man, grabbed presumably for something to help but got instead the scarf and jerked it out of the man's hand. Harvey then miraculously regained his balance, stuffed the scarf into his shirt, and began mumbling something vaguely apologetic, vaguely Lakota Sioux, perhaps even vaguely a little under the influence of alcohol. The two men were huffing and puffing, cussing, trying to stand, starting to come for Harvey. But there were others there--race officials who were watching the turn, and two of them came toward the scuffle.

"Break it up, folks. Just watch the race. No rough stuff." One of the race officials took Harvey by the arm and ushered him to the outer edge of the few folks watching the turn. Harvey watched it as well. The poker horse was ahead; the bay didn't make a quick turn, but the other two horses did fine. The poker horse would need to get a good lead before he started to tire; the bay would be able to make up a lot of distance with his long stride and his apparent ability to go long. But at this point, it would be a more fairly run race, in Harvey's view. No injury or spooking of the lead horse at the turn. Brady would later call Harvey's actions "Injun-uity"--not in an insulting way. Harvey tolerated the joke with wry patience.

The poker horse did win; Brady did collect a little cash, but the odds weren't good. He split the meager winnings with Harvey, who tucked the little bit away in one of his little pouches. The bay came in second and looked as if he could have gone another round--not any quicker but with little more effort.

The poker horse cowboy came up to Harvey at the livery after the race.

"Friend, you saved us all. This race could have been the end of all four horses, not to mention the riders."

Harvey ducked a little, shrugged and nodded.

"This means I get to keep this horse. I won enough to pay my poker debt--and I have a little extra I'd like to give you as a thank-you for saving maybe all of us in the race." Harvey declined the cash but accepted the cowboy's hand, then moved off to the rear of the livery. Brady and the cowboy chatted for just a few more minutes, reviewing Harvey's actions. The cowboy said he'd emptied his canteen of the questionable contents but that he didn't know who'd sabotaged his saddle. He also didn't know the men Harvey had boonswoggled. The cowboy again expressed his thanks and left. Then Brady joined Harvey in the shade.

"Nice job, Harvey."

Harvey shrugged.

Chapter 17

The race of the day before had put extra excitement in their day, and Brady, Oscar and Harvey all rested well. In the morning, Brady explained to Harvey his idea about the shack Duke and Cora had used and what he planned to do. Harvey nodded once. While Brady investigated the shack, Harvey would go back in the saloon and listen. If the horses with the two dead outlaws had come back to town, there would be talk of it. If not, the death of the miner who had been shot by the boy would be big news by itself. Everyone in town would be talking and adding their ideas to the story.

The shack was even worse than Brady had imagined. Sagging porch, shingles loose on the roof, some scattered around on the ground. Window boarded up, door not closed tightly. The inside was no better. Cora didn't seem to be much for keeping house. Dirty dishes, a few clothes on the floor, a few papers on the table. It looked as if they had left in such a big hurry they didn't take time to pack everything.

Brady picked up the papers and spread them all out on the table. There were notes on the price of cattle, a couple that looked like land prices. One paper in particular caught his interest. It was a page from a newspaper in Casper, Wyoming Territory. A big ad touted the opportunities available in that area. Coal mines needed workers. The vast range land offered ranchers a chance to raise cattle and sheep. Brady stopped breathing for a moment at the next line: Plans for the expansion of railroads in the area were being worked on! He just looked at the paper; there was no doubt Duke and Cora were headed for Casper! It was big enough to be anonymous in; there was land to be had by legal means or otherwise. Brady had no doubt they would be more likely to take the land by cheating a homesteader than buying it. They had plans to be big ranchers; they could do it out there...in any number of ways.

A brief thought of Sullie's other brother, Dan, crossed

Brady's mind. Duke and Cora probably wouldn't include Dan in their big plans. Dan had seemed almost meek in comparison to Duke. No question: Duke had always called the shots at their place. Dan would probably not be included in their new plans. Brady would have to deal with Dan when he returned home.

It made sense that Duke and Cora had left the settlement headed to the southwest. The first big settlement would be Casper. After that, if they continued on south, there would be Cheyenne, also a booming town and cattle country, and the railroad came through there. Denver, the largest city, was a little farther south than Cheyenne. Brady thought about their choices and decided they would probably stake their chances on the nearest big town, Casper. Cora wouldn't put up with a long, hard trip. She would want to get somewhere quickly where they could not be found, and they could settle down. He was sure she would assume Brady would have given up looking for them. Cora always thought she was smarter than everyone else and wouldn't think she and Duke were at risk.

Brady looked around the shack a little more, but didn't find anything else useful. He shook his head ruefully. Duke and Cora saw themselves as cattle barons; instead, they had been chased to this dirty, run-down shack and the rough settlement, and now were on the run again. They would never acknowledge that their problems were their own fault--not Brady's and Sullie's or old Marsh's or anyone else they blamed.

* * *

Harvey was loading their supplies into packs. He hadn't heard much useful talk except one miner who bragged long and loud that he'd seen a man and woman high-tailing it out of town, and that had to be who killed the man. Harvey shook his head. "Man has too much beer, too much talk, not enough smart."

Brady laughed. Harvey was right. The man would keep telling his story, others would add their own bigger and better version, and soon the boy would be forgotten.

They decided it would be better to leave early in the morning, take this last evening to be sure all their rigging and equipment were in good shape and to be sure they had enough supplies. They were headed into country where it could become cold quickly; it was important to be prepared for anything.

Harvey's people had given him much information about trails through Paha Sapa, the best ways to cross the mountains, places to camp, and places to look out for ambush. There was a wagon road that led west to Wyoming Territory. It would be the easiest route out of the mountains. But if Duke and Cora suspected they were followed, it would also afford the best places to stage an ambush.

The sky was barely light as they drank a quick cup of coffee, ate a piece of jerky, and finished packing all their equipment. Oscar got his piece of jerky and a biscuit. Crossing the mountains would be hard work for him.

The sun was just touching the lowest peaks as they left the settlement. They had followed the road for an hour or more when Harvey pointed to a slight track off the road to the left. He turned Old Horse onto it and started through the trees. All day they moved along a faint trail Brady often could not see. As usual, Harvey seemed to know just where he wanted to go and followed the faint trail without hesitation.

Oscar began to fall behind as they went up and down steep slopes. Harvey stopped and lifted the old dog onto his horse. Oscar gave him a grateful look and settled comfortably into his place at the front of the make-shift saddle.

By late afternoon the hills were not as high or steep and the going became easier. "Find road tomorrow. No more mountains," Harvey said.

They found a small stream and made camp for the night. There was a little grass for the horses and trees that would prevent them from being seen. It was a familiar routine: Unsaddle, build a fire and cook some food, then roll up in the blankets for the night. It was chilly in the mountains, so Oscar curled up close to Harvey, gave a loud sigh, and fell asleep.

Daylight found them on the trail again the next morning. In a few hours, they had moved out of the mountains and were crossing a vast, rugged, treeless prairie. Long stretches of flat grassland ended in abrupt drop-offs into deep canyons. Bare buttes rose occasionally from the land. It was like nothing Brady had seen before. Sometimes there would be a small stream or spring at the base of a sheer cliff, surrounded by a few trees and grass. They saw a couple of sheepherders' wagons in the distance but stayed far away.

"Sheep wild, run. Smell bad," Harvey said.

There were cattle, also, scattered over the prairie. The days all had the same pattern--up early, eat, saddle up. move out. They rode steadily, always watching to avoid places someone could lay in wait for them. They talked little. Harvey picked up Oscar more frequently to let him rest. Crossing the mountains, the frequent up-and-down steep slopes, had been hard on him, and his limp had become more pronounced. When they came upon a stream with plenty of grass, they would stop early to give the horses some rest and a good feeding.

Mid-afternoon they spotted cattle grazing in a broad valley, a single rider near them. They turned to ride in that direction. As they neared the man, they noticed that he looked tense and his hand was near his gun. Before they got too close to him, Brady called out.

"Saw you out here and stopped to say hello." They moved nearer. "I'm Brady Quillan. This is Harvey Two Shirts. We're just passing by. This your place?"

The cowboy nodded. "Jim Hedman," the man replied. "Yeah, this is mine."

"Nice country," Brady said. "Can see why you would choose it. Good pasture land."

Jim smiled and nodded. He looked friendlier and his hand was not so near his gun. "Where you two headed?"

"Down toward Casper. Been following a couple of people, and they seem to be going that way. Got business with them. Have you seen any strangers besides us recently?"

Jim's smile disappeared and he hesitated a moment before he answered. "A man and a woman came through couple days ago. They stopped by the house and asked for some water." He squinted, shook his head, then continued. "No, they didn't ask. They TOLD us they were getting water for them and their horses out of our pump. They seemed mean. Awful unpleasant pair." He adjusted his hat. "My wife, Millie, asked the woman if she'd like to come in for a few minutes and get out of the sun. That woman looked down her nose at my wife and said she wasn't going into any squatter's shack. They got some water and left. I had the feeling if I hadn't been there, something bad would have happened." It was obvious the insult and the possible danger had left him shaken.

Brady listened grimly. He was right that Duke and Cora were headed for Casper. He felt sure that the Hedmans would have been in a great deal of danger if Duke and Cora had not wanted to reach Casper before making any move to acquire land.

"Bad people, trouble," Harvey said, very quietly.

"Yes," Brady nodded, "really bad. They have killed several people, and we have a personal score to settle. They are cold-blooded killers. It was a mighty good thing you were holding that gun." He picked up his reins, preparing to leave. "Keep a watch, but I don't think they'll be back this way. Thanks for the information. We'll be heading on down that way. They can't keep running forever."

"Watch your back. They seemed like the kind that wouldn't mind shooting someone from behind," Jim cautioned, and raised his hand in farewell as they turned south again and rode on.

* * *

The days wore on. Their life had acquired a routine, and there was little need for talk. Both men understood what they would be up against when they finally confronted Duke and Cora.

They saw ranches more frequently as they neared Casper. The going became easier when they found a road leading in that direction. It seemed to be a main road across the territory. Wagons and riders were headed in each direction.

The mountains loomed in the distance. A rider who stopped to talk with them described Casper as a busy town, right at the bottom of a mountain. Ranching was the main business in the whole area. Lots of cattle and sheep were shipped east by rail from the town.

"Most of the livestock are being shipped by one ranch," the cowboy told them. "It's getting to be pretty big. They've bought up some of the smaller places, but there are still several ranches in the area. It's good country to raise cattle, and if you're looking for work, it's good country to find it in."

Brady and Harvey visited with him a little. The cowboy was talkative and gladly shared all he knew about the territory and people. There were mostly ranchers and ranch hands, miners, and railroad people. Cattle and coal were shipped from there; Casper was a booming town.

The mountain dominated the horizon. Casper lay at the base and spread onto the surrounding prairie.

Their first stop was at a livery stable. The horses needed rest and food. Oscar had ridden with Harvey for several hours and needed a chance to stretch out and lie down.

A tall, gray-haired man met them at the barn door. "Bob Hinkley," he said, extending his hand. "What can I do for you?"

Brady shook hands and introduced himself and Harvey. "We need to put up our horses. Need a stall and some feed and water. The dog can stay in a stall with them if that's all right. He's no bother."

Bob showed them stalls and where to get hay and water for the horses, then leaned over to pet Oscar. "He can rest right here with me," the old man said. "I miss having a dog around since mine died. I'll get him water and I might even have a bone he can gnaw on." Brady knew Oscar wouldn't give the man any trouble. He made friends instantly, wherever they were.

"Is there a sheriff here in town?" Brady asked. He had looked at as much of the town as could be seen from the livery stable, but there were many side streets and it wasn't possible to see all of it.

"Yes, indeed. Go on down that road you came in on. It's several blocks down, across from that big hotel sticking up in the air." He gestured in the direction of the tallest building on the main road.

Casper had a wide variety of stores and offices all along the road. General stores, diners, saloons, law offices, coal mine offices, hotels, a doctor's office, and, beyond the business district, a church was visible. Men and women hurried along the sidewalks, in and out of businesses. Wagons rumbled up the streets, some pulled by oxen, most pulled by teams of horses. Farther down the street, a stagecoach stood waiting as a few passengers boarded. As they watched the activity, a train whistle could be heard in the distance. Casper was indeed the center of activity in the Territory.

Harvey planned to just drift along the street. He would not be noticed but usually would hear or see something of interest to them. Brady strode off toward the sheriff's office.

The sheriff was sitting at his desk, leaned back in his chair with his eyes closed when Brady opened the door. Brady paused for a moment, not wanting to startle the sheriff awake, but the sheriff chuckled and spoke without opening his eyes. "Come on in. I was just taking a break. The town's quiet today. Might as well get a nap when I can."

"You've got the right idea. You probably never know for sure when you'll get another chance." Brady smiled. "I'm Brady Quillan. My partner and I just got to town. We've been trailing a couple of people who seemed to be headed this way. I wondered if you might have any information about them. Names are Duke and Cora Marsh. From over in Dakota Territory."

"Nice to meet you. I'm Lester Stokes. Why you asking about them?"

"Well, he's wanted for murder, killed a family member. I've got a personal score to settle with him. He's been involved in at least one other murder." Brady adjusted his hat. "I'm not sure his wife has done any killing herself, but she is right there with him every time." He paused to collect his thoughts.

Sheriff Stokes shuffled through some papers on his desk. "I had a notice to be on the lookout for a couple, no names, wanted by the US marshal. That could be them." He leaned back again, looking closely at Brady. "You aren't law enforcement, are you? What's the story?"

Brady hesitated a moment before replying. "The family member he killed was his sister, my wife. She had been willed a large section of the family ranch by their father. That property combined with my place made a mighty fine ranch, good cattle country. Duke and Cora Marsh thought they deserved it all, decided to take it one way or another." Brady preferred to keep his explanation short, few details. There was no way to express the loss of Sullie and of their dreams. It was better if he offered only the bare facts and not let the grief and anger overwhelm the story.

"A couple came into town a few days ago. Heard they were asking about land available to settle on. Everything in the Territory has pretty much been claimed, so not much to start a real operation. But I also heard that one of the biggest ranches around was for sale. Water and plenty of land for pasture and to put up hay. Real pretty country, west of the mountain. Extends into the reservation." His chair squeaked as he leaned forward to continue. "It's owned by a foreigner, Englishman, I think. Last I heard he'd had enough of the winters around here and wanted to get rid of the place. It's outside my jurisdiction so I've never been out there myself." The sheriff stopped talking, waited to see if Brady was thinking the same thing he was.

The only sound in the room for several minutes was the ticking of the clock on the shelf.

Finally Brady began talking again. "Yeah, that sounds like something they'd be interested in. They probably wouldn't intend to buy it but would try to cheat their way into owning it. If the owner isn't around anymore, no one would know the ownership status when he left the country. I guess it'd depend on how many hands he left to run things after he left."

"How about a cup of coffee while we think on this?" The sheriff got up and began to pour two cups. "What are you planning to do if they're there, if you catch up with them?"

Brady sat down, took some deep breaths. It didn't seem possible they had finally caught up with Duke and Cora. He considered his answer to the sheriff carefully. It wouldn't be smart to seem like a hot-head who would shoot anyone in order to get revenge on Duke and Cora.

"Well, I want to see them pay for what they did. I'd like to see them stand trial, spend their lives in prison. If I catch up to them, we'll try to capture them. But if they want a fight, they'll get one." Brady hoped his answer was just vague enough to sound like he'd first try to capture them peaceably. The sheriff sat quietly, then indicated he'd trust Brady to act with caution and stay within the law. They'd both be nervous about what the outcome of confronting Duke would be.

They talked for a while longer about the ranch, the best trail to get there. The sheriff described the country as similar to what they had come across already. There was a road leading west, a small settlement on the reservation. The headquarters of the ranch lay on the border of the reservation. The sheriff had heard there was a large log house, barns and corrals. The Englishman had put a lot into building a fine ranch. It ran over a thousand head of cattle, and he shipped every year from Casper. There were ranch hands, but only a couple lived full-time at the headquarters.

Brady thanked the sheriff for the coffee and information and said they'd be heading out toward the ranch. "I hope we can get there and keep that owner from having a problem. One way or another, we'll stop back by and let you know what we run into."

"Thanks. I'd appreciate that. Good luck out there." The sheriff stood, and they shook hands.

Harvey was waiting for him across the street when Brady left the sheriff's office. Brady relayed the information he had gotten from the sheriff as they started back toward the livery stable. They would take food back with them. The stable would be a more private place to plan their next move.

They stepped into the street, paused a moment to let a buggy pass. Brady was not thinking of the people in the buggy but glanced up as it passed. The shock took a moment to register. The woman in the buggy was Cora! They recognized each other at the same time. "NO! Get out of here, fast," she shouted to the man beside her. The man was startled, too, but responded quickly. They sped away, Cora's yellow shawl and the man's red shirt tail flapping.

Brady was speechless. Harvey grunted. The man with Cora was not Duke. They both spun around, looking every direction to see if Duke were close by. The buggy was moving fast, and no one was following it. It seemed like maybe Duke was not in town. No words were spoken but Brady and Harvey both knew they had to follow that buggy. They hurried to the livery stable to get the horses, saddled as quickly as possible, and headed up the road in the direction the buggy had gone. It was nowhere in sight.

Several roads led out of town. "Which way?" Brady asked.

Harvey thought for a few seconds. "Ranch that way. Maybe hide, not go right there." Brady nodded. It made sense that Cora would not want to be followed. They could easily have stopped out of sight in town and would take another route back to the Englishman's big ranch.....if they were even really going to the ranch.

The horses moved off at a brisk walk. They felt good after their brief rest, moving quickly through the streets, soon reaching the edge of town. Oscar trotted behind. Suddenly Harvey stopped and pointed. "Buggy there. They ride horses now." Brady looked closely at the buggy; Harvey was right. The buggy had been abandoned, the horses were gone. They must be riding and could make much better time.

"We have to take a chance that the ranch is where we'll find them," Brady said. "Let's try to get there before they do."

Harvey nodded, got off and picked up Oscar. They planned to travel fast, so Oscar needed to be carried. They'd be going across more rough country and had only a vague notion of where they were headed. Brady appreciated Harvey as a partner even more than usual just now. Harvey always had the packs and supplies ready to go quickly if needed. They hadn't had to waste any time getting ready, just saddled, loaded their equipment and headed out.

The ranch was a long day's ride from town. It was late afternoon when they had ridden out of town. The country was unfamiliar to them; they decided it would be safer to camp that night and move on in the morning. Brady hoped Cora would think they had no idea where to go, wouldn't be headed toward the big ranch. Duke would be a different story. He would be thinking like an outlaw--a desperate, dangerous outlaw.

Their camp was made in a shallow gully, their firepit small and low. They hobbled the horses, boiled their coffee, and ate what little dried food they had. Oscar seemed plenty satisfied with a piece of jerky, a couple of chunks of bacon, and a small slab of cold frybread.

They had finished their last cup of strong coffee. It was quiet, no wind. It was cold as could be, and they huddled close to the fire, blankets held tightly around their shoulders. Harvey squirmed a bit, then spoke.

"You remember I told you about the lady who taught me to write?"

Brady nodded.

"She taught me many things." He squirmed a bit more, adjusted his blanket. "I can speak just like you, like other white men. Not in the Indian way."

It caught Brady off guard.

"Harvey! What are you sayin'? "

Harvey didn't respond.

"Why in the hell have you been talking Indian English all this time? Without telling me?" Harvey remained silent.

"We've been together weeks! And mostly you just grunt. Or point. Or nod. You use chopped off pieces of talk." Brady couldn't believe what Harvey was admitting. He knew he was sputtering. It was unbelievable that Harvey could have kept up this kind of --what? almost a disguise--for weeks.

"You must realize it is easier for me to speak with few words. And with most people, it is best that I seem ignorant." Harvey's voice was clear but very quiet. "My own language has few of the extras you use in your English. It's easy for me to leave off the extras when I speak English." He stirred the fire a bit. "I am sorry if this seems...dishonest to you. I have done this with good intention, not bad."

"Hell, Harvey. I guess I see what you mean. But all this time!! I can hardly believe it." Brady shook his head back and forth, stretched out a leg and gouged the dirt with his heel. "When we've been in bad situations, it seems like you'd have spoken in white man's English."

"That's when it's most important I speak with few words, don't you see?"

"You've been my closest partner. My closest friend. And I didn't even know how you really are."

"You know how I am." Harvey poked the fire. "You just didn't know how I could speak."

Brady thought that over. It was true. Harvey Two Shirts was the most honest, ethical, trustworthy, clear-thinking man he knew. Not to mention the bravest, most compassionate, most helpful. And the best cook of frybread in bleak circumstances. A deep breath, and Brady was ready to move on to another thought. They were actually having a conversation! Speaking in sentences, not nods and shrugs! It had been good for Brady to cut down on his chatter, probably. He knew he wasted time and words occasionally. But what a fine experience to hear Harvey speaking this way! He had already known Harvey was exceptionally intelligent; but something about hearing him speak in complete sentences emphasized that intelligence. That was surely a biased view, Brady admitted to himself. But damn if it wasn't so. He knew now that his plan for an emergency would be more acceptable to the few other people involved.

"Harvey, we'll prob'ly meet up with Duke and Cora tomorrow first thing. And it's prob'ly gonna be rough. We might get hurt or even killed." They had already discussed this, briefly. But Brady wanted to emphasize the danger. Wanted to make his next statements sink in.

"Here's a letter I want you to hang on to for me. If things don't go well and I don't make it through tomorrow, you do whatever you need to to keep yourself safe. And try to get back to my place. It's way over east from where I found you, but you can ask around and find it." He stopped for a breath. Harvey was watching him intently.

"Tassle will be at the Marsh place. You can trust him. Give him this letter. It says you can live in my house as long as you want and that half the land at my old place will be yours. He will help you get cash when you need it at the bank." Another pause. This was difficult for Brady Quillan. The only other person he'd ever trusted this completely was Sullie.

Harvey didn't speak for a while, then stood. "You honor me, Brady Quillan." He made a slight bow, then sat back down. "You must know, my friend, that it's not common for an Indian to own land. There may be problems. I do not need land to be complete. I have people in many places, and I will never starve. And now I will tell you a thing."

He was silent another moment, then spoke with the confidence of an orator telling of past history. "You remember when we first met, I told you I would tell your name one day. I have thought many times about that." As he spoke, he looked off toward the way they had come. "You are like the big river. I have seen you bright, like stars showing in the water. I have seen you quiet and smooth, and I have seen you help move people along. I have seen you angry, like dark water crashing against the shore." He took a deep breath, then continued. "I have known that beneath the surface, there is much more to be seen. Like the river, you have many changes. Many levels." He stirred the fire again.

"I have thought about this much. I have considered many river names. And I have chosen the best name." He looked directly at Brady.

"The name for you is...Brady Quillan." His voice then quieted. "And I am proud to be your friend these many weeks and for many more."

Brady stood then, approached Harvey and shook his hand. "You honor me, Harvey Two Shirts."

Chapter 18

It was still dark when they mounted their horses, Oscar riding with Harvey, and they moved out. A piece of jerky for each one and a drink of water were breakfast. They pushed the horses faster than usual but knew it was necessary. The ranch came into view in the distance in the early afternoon. The house and barns were on a high, flat area at the base of a low mountain. The main house sat apart a short distance from a smaller house and the barns. Both houses were surrounded by several big shade trees. More trees shaded parts of the barns and corrals. A road led up a long hill and then flattened out the rest of the way to the buildings. There were several rock outcroppings among the trees, an especially large one a short distance from the front of the big house. Harvey nodded toward it, a frown on his face. Brady understood immediately--it was a perfect place for a gunman or two, with a view of the house as well as trails in and out.

Trees and low brush dotted the landscape. Brady and Harvey stopped in a stand of trees a distance from the buildings. They could see horses in the corral, and a woman walking between the main house and the smaller one. Brady was studying the ranch with binoculars.

"Okay, there she is. Cora. I don't think they could know we're here." Brady was partly talking to Harvey and partly thinking out loud. "I hope we're in time and the owner isn't dead." Harvey squinted at the layout and nodded.

"I get close, go to rocks. You go to house." Harvey pointed which direction each would head. It made sense to Brady. He would approach from the front, and with luck would not be seen until he was very close.

Harvey rode on up the draw, out of the line of sight of the buildings. He turned toward the big rock outcropping, stopped in a stand of trees just at the edge. He left his horse tied in the trees, and he and Oscar began to slip quietly into the rocks. He hadn't moved far when he caught a glimpse of movement ahead. A dark jacket and hat, sunlight glinting off a rifle barrel. The man was moving quickly, scaling the sharp edge of a large slanted slab of granite. Harvey could hear the man's boots scrape on the rocks; his own footsteps were silent as he moved quickly to follow, Oscar close at his side. As he slid quietly around another huge rock, he stopped in his tracks: Duke Marsh was just ahead, opposite the man in the dark jacket, his back toward them. Oscar made a low snarl, and Duke turned quickly, his pistol in hand. A shot rang out, then another. Oscar went down, Harvey stumbled and fell. Two more shots came from the direction of the ranch house. Harvey was in pain, but was able to crawl toward where he'd seen Duke.

Duke's voice bellowed out from the rocks. "Is that you, Quillan? Come on out and face me like a man!" Duke moved through the rocks, toward the near side of the big house. "I already shot your Injun and that mangy dog of yours. Now I'll get you."

Shots rang out from two directions. Harvey heard ricochets from the rocks above him, then Brady's voice. "Duke, you're a thief and a murderer, You're gonna go to jail or die, whichever works best for you." Harvey heard a scramble of boots on rock, then hoofbeats. He crawled over a ledge and saw two horsemen galloping toward the trail leading into the ranch. Even from a distance, he could identify one as the man who was with Cora in town, the red shirt. Marsh's outlaws were deserting him. There was no loyalty here.

"Don't talk so big, Quillan. You squatted on my land and now you don't have anything." Duke was moving closer to the house after each outburst. "I'm the oldest son, I have the right to all of it. You don't have no rights at all. And you warped my sister's mind." Duke had balanced his pistol on top of a rock ledge.

Harvey heard Brady's voice again, sounding more clearly. "Come on out, Duke. I'll take you in to jail. Cora, too. That'll be your best deal."

"Forget it, Quillan." And Duke shot toward the house. More shots came toward the rock pile, and Harvey heard a grunt as one found its mark on Duke Marsh. He crawled forward, his leg leaving a trail of blood on the rocks. Duke was lying on his back, blood starting to seep up on the front of his jacket. He was still breathing, but the location of the blood looked as if the wound might be fatal. Harvey crawled closer, eased up to a sitting position beside Duke Marsh.

"I think you are done for, Duke Marsh." Harvey spoke quietly. "It is good. Gunshot. Jail. It is one. Same. You die."

Duke's eyelids fluttered, then he stared at Harvey. "You worthless trash Injun.... You're spose to be dead.... I shot you." He winced, grunted. Then his head fell to the side and he made no more movement. Harvey made no response to Duke's last words. He simply struggled to return to where Oscar lay.

There were more shots from close to the house. Harvey figured Cora must be shooting at Brady, Brady returning the fire. But Harvey's first concern now was to help Oscar. He continued dragging his injured leg toward the crevice in the rocks where Duke's shots had hit their marks.

Brady had moved quickly toward the ranch buildings, working his way carefully toward the back door, expecting to hear gunfire any moment. There had been no more sound from the rockpile, and he figured Harvey and Oscar had been able to take care of Duke. Winchester in hand, Brady stepped up onto the back porch, pushed open the door, found himself in a big kitchen. Cora was sitting in a chair, hands tied behind her, cursing and trying to get loose.

"Hold it right there. Drop your gun," a voice ordered. Startled, Brady did as he was ordered. Then he noticed the badge on the man's chest--the circled star. U.S. Marshal. "What? What? What's going on?"

"I'm the marshal in this territory. What are you doing here? And YOU tell ME what's going on. You're Brady Quillan, right? Why'd you shoot Duke Marsh?"-

"Sir? Marshal? Surprised to see you here." He stood straight, wishing he had his Winchester at his side.

The marshal stepped back."Well, we've been keepin' an eye on you for a while, Brady Quillan. You and your pal. We know of some ruckuses you've been involved in--and we've heard of some you get the blame for that you might not have had anything to do with." The corners of his mouth turned down, but not in anger or disgust; more like wry humor. "But we've kept an eye on Duke and Cora Marsh, too. We heard early on about the killing of your wife, then of several other questionable events. We've been trailing them for quite a while."

"Sir, thank you, sir. I'll be glad to answer any questions. But I need to get up in the rock pile and check on my partner and my dog. And I guess Duke Marsh."

"I understand," the marshal replied. "I'll go with you. I think we'll be finding Duke Marsh's body." He glanced toward Cora. "Sorry, ma'am. But that's a criminal's end result." Cora moaned, gasped, sobbed, then shrieked. "GODDAMN YOU ALL! GODDAMN YOU ALL TO HELL!" The marshal faced Brady again and continued. "Cora Marsh will go back with me to Casper to jail. There is considerable cause for an extended jail term. She'll be just fine here until we get back from the rockpile."

It didn't take Brady and the marshal long to find Harvey and Oscar. Harvey was in obvious pain but had tied a bandana around his thigh and was trying to stand. Brady helped him up. Harvey's voice was strained. "It is bad for Oscar."

"We'll take care of him, Harvey. You just try to get back down toward the house." The marshal supported him as they made their way back through the rocks. Brady lifted Oscar and followed behind. The dog's body was limp, his eyes were closed. Blood dripped from a wound behind his shoulder, but he was breathing. Thank God he was breathing.

They stumbled into the yard in front of the big house. The marshal helped Harvey to a seat on the porch step, then said, "I'll go back to get Duke. I can do it alone. You guys take care of your wounds." As the marshal turned away to get his horse, Brady turned first toward Harvey. "How about your leg, Harvey? You gonna be okay?"

""Okay. Will use good powder. We need to check Oscar."

They knelt by Oscar, one on each side. Oscar still had not moved, and his breathing was shallow, irregular. The wound was bad, behind and below the shoulder. Oscar's eyes were unfocused; he made no sound.

"It is bad. Oscar will not live." Harvey's voice was solemn. "It was my purpose to care for Oscar. I have failed."

Brady's grief was severe but he knew there was no failure on the part of Harvey. "No, Harvey. No failure. We both are responsible for including Oscar in all we did."

Oscar made a slight sound. Not a whimper, not a groan. Simply an exhalation. Brady and Harvey each had a hand on Oscar. They felt the life leave him. Neither man could look at the other; for each, the grief was too intense .

They stayed that way for several minutes. Then Harvey stood.

"It is not the way of my people to honor dog. We honor eagle. Buffalo. Bear. Elk. Owl. Not dog." His face was gray, his eyes darkened. He stood over Oscar, rubbing his calloused hands, then made waving gestures in the air, side to side, then up and down.

"Harvey, what are you doing?" Brady was barely aware of Harvey's movements, but he knew something was going on.

"It is the way we honor the dead." Facing the south, he rubbed the palms of his hands together again, steadily. "It is the sound of the wind blowing the prairie grasses." He gracefully moved his hands to the west in a slow, sweeping movement.

He turned to the west. "It is the sound of the rains falling on the forest leaves." He raised his hands, then let them fall, his fingers moving slightly, fluttering.

Facing the north, he continued. "It is the sound of the snow blowing across the frozen ground." And his arms moved forward and back, forward and back, then in a swirl.

Then, face toward the east, he tilted his head and continued. "It is the sound of the water, rushing over the rocks in the stream." He took a deep breath then, and continued, his voice calm.

"This is the sound that is always with us. It is the way we remember...and honor...the dead." Harvey continued rubbing his leathery hands together, then his humming began.

And then it became a keening, still soft, but in the manner of his people, he grieved aloud and asked for comfort for Oscar on his journey to the spirit land.

After a while, Harvey faced Brady. "I ask your permission to take Oscar now. I know your heart is sad. My heart is sad, also." He paused. "But Oscar was in my care. I will care for him now."

Brady nodded; his heart was sad, for sure. His throat and chest hurt, his stomach was tight. His eyes were wet. He nodded again. It was almost beyond him to take the final steps for this great dog. He trusted Harvey with the care of Oscar, knowing it would be the right thing.

"I will come for you when I am ready," Harvey said quietly. "It will be by sundown."

Brady went back to the barn yard, close to the big house. He sat on an overturned bucket and thought back on all the times he and Oscar had shared. First just the two of them. Then with Sullie, with Tassle, finally with Harvey. At the last, with Harvey. He remembered the Badlands, with Oscar peering out from Harvey's jacket and blanket. Following along behind the makeshift travois. Resting beside Harvey when Harvey had been beaten. So many, many memorable times. And finally, the brave Oscar, facing their enemy with courage and determination. Giving his life for their long and difficult goal: To avenge the death of one who loved him unconditionally. To aid Brady in that almost impossible goal. The lump in Brady's throat grew. This was too hard.

More than two hours passed as Brady sat on the bucket, walked a bit around the barnyard, searched the sky, worried about Harvey's wound as he cared for Oscar. There were no hands from the big ranch to disturb him. Only one person intruded on his thoughts: The marshal came by, leading two horses--one with Cora, one with the body of Duke Marsh.

"I won't need to see you again until you come back by on your way to Dakota Territory. I'll see you around the settlement. No need to worry. You and Harvey Two Shirts will be okay with the law." Cora had looked only at her hands tied to the saddle horn. She made no sound. They left, heading east.

Brady did not watch them leave.

It was clouding up a bit; the sun was moving toward the west. Finally Harvey came. He motioned for Brady to come with him, then moved back toward the riverside. From a short distance, right at the edge of the reservation, overlooking the river, Brady saw what Harvey had constructed: It was the burial platform.

High above the prairie grass, Oscar lay on the platform. It was well over Brady's head, but from the distance, he could see Oscar's body lay with his nose pointed to the east. There was an eagle feather, some beads. And Harvey's new shirt draped over Oscar's shoulders, covering his wound. The tin pie plate was there, too, with a lump of frybread and a strip of beef. Brady could only nod and touch the shoulder of his friend.

They stood together for some time, each with his own thoughts. It would be hard for Brady to leave Oscar here, to know he'd probably never be this close again. He'd only felt this depth of grief once before, and that was for Sullie. She would have grieved as deeply as Brady did, he knew. And the same was true for Harvey. Harvey had honored Oscar in the finest way possible. That memory would be with Brady forever.

* * *

Finally the two friends turned away from the burial platform.

"Harvey, we're through here. We have a long way to go to make it home."

"This is true."

"The horses are plumb wore out. What do you think about catching the cattle train back to the settlement?"

Harvey looked startled. "Train?" He looked intently at Brady. "I maybe don't trust train."

"Oh, a train is safe alright. They haul people and cattle and ore and lumber. All the time. No problem."

They had seen a few trains and many miles of track around the settlement and on into Wyoming. The tracks went all the way into the territory and down into Sioux City, close to Brady's ranch. Well, maybe not close, but at least within riding distance.

"Let's ride back toward Casper and see about how much it would cost. Take a look at the cattle cars. Check about hay and feed for the trip. See how long it would take to get to the settlement, then maybe check on picking it up later to get the rest of the way. Maybe it even comes close to Mount Alta, where I picked you up." It was only weeks, but it seemed like a long time ago.

Harvey grumbled. Change wasn't easy for him. Particularly when it involved something so big, so loud, so intimidating.

They rode into Casper, stopped briefly at the sheriff's office to let him know about the events at the big ranch and the involvement of the marshal, then headed for the train station. There was an engine with a long line of cars on the track, and they were able to see cattle being loaded from the pens beside the track. It was loud--not noise from the train but from the cattle bawling and men hollering. They rode away from the big train, back toward the station. Brady handed his reins to Harvey and went inside the station. It wasn't long before he came back, having learned the train would indeed go into the settlement. It would be a fairly short trip and was affordable. Hay was available nearby, and they could load right away. The train was scheduled to leave in just a couple of hours. The tricky thing would be to convince Harvey this was the thing to do. Brady figured it would be better for Harvey's wound to ride in a cattle car instead of on horseback. Harvey had used his nameless powder on the wound, and it looked good to Brady. But...anything to help it heal faster...

They led the horses around in front of the big engine, then down alongside the cars. Both horses seemed calm, not spooked by either the machine or the bawling cattle already loaded. They came to an empty car. The doors were already slid open, so they could peer inside. There was much more room inside than it seemed there would be, from the outside. Plenty of space. They'd need to get buckets for water, arrange for hay to be delivered. But the floor of the car wasn't too dirty. They'd slept in worse places, for sure.

Harvey grunted again. "This will save much time. If we make it alive."

"Don't worry, Harvey. We'll make it. Let's get busy gettin' ready." Convincing Harvey was easier than he thought it would be.

It took less than an hour to make the arrangements. A ramp was ready for them to load the horses, and neither horse gave them a problem. The horses were tied to rings in the wall of the car. It was dark inside when the doors slid shut, and Brady was wondering if they still had fuel for the lantern in the pack. Too late now to think about it. They'd ride in the dark if necessary; made resting easier. They brushed loose hay out of the way, then put their bedrolls against the front wall of the car. They peered through the cracks in the sides of the car to watch activity at the station, watched more loading, brushed the horses, keeping an ear out for signs of the engine coming to life. No idea of how the horses would react to steam hissing, the loud chug of the engine. But there were no problems at all. Brady figured tired horses were plenty easy to look after. Harvey was not as tense, either--maybe tired humans were easier, too.

They stood beside the horses as the engine pulled out of the station, but soon went back to the front of the car and sat on their bedrolls. It would be just a few hours until they reached the settlement. Much easier than the horseback ride would have been.

Brady felt the exhaustion--not just the long, long ride, but the emotional toll from tracking, dealing with the outlaws, confronting Duke, the loss of Oscar, Harvey's wound--it left him almost limp. But there was satisfaction there, below the anxiety and grief. He felt a calm that was new. Not since he'd been at home with Sullie still alive had he felt this quiet peace. He was tired. But satisfied. Now to get home; check on things at the ranch, get Harvey to wherever he was going. The road ahead was long but not threatening. Harvey had two words for it: ahbanah and ahbahyenah--calm and quiet.

Chapter 19

It was night when they reached the settlement. The train station was not far from the main road through town. They unloaded the horses, saddled and packed up their gear, rode to the livery. Zach wasn't there, but they knew it would be okay to move into the stalls at the rear of the livery. They filled the water pails, helped themselves to Zach's feed and hay. The horses would be stiff for a while--bracing against the occasional swaying of the railroad car was an unusual movement for them, and they'd used muscles not ordinarily used. They snorted and stomped in the stalls, obviously feeling at home again. The diner would be closed, but the saloon would have something for them to eat. Brady walked up the street to see what he could find.

Good old beef sandwiches--it hurt his heart not to order one for Oscar--and a couple of apples made a decent meal. Harvey's leg was better after his rest on the train, and he moved around well. They'd spend a day here, refitting gear, replenishing supplies. Brady included two new leather shirts for Harvey from the store, asked if the owner had heard anything about Richard. No recent word--which was good news.

It was a difficult thing for Brady to answer Zach's inquiry about where Oscar was. Much easier to relate the events of their confrontation with Duke and Cora. Zach would be eager to spread the word of that event to his cronies in the settlement.

One restful extra day at the livery, and then Brady and Harvey left, headed for home. It would be a long ride, but they'd eventually pick up the train again to give themselves and the horses an easier trip.

They traveled far but quickly. The horses did well. The weather was cold but dry. They left the hilly part of Paha Sapa and were soon making good progress toward the Badlands. As they came up over a rise that looked familiar to Brady, he turned to Harvey. "I'd like to stop by that Ballard place. Maybe we can spend the night there. A nice little lady. Feisty but nice."

Harvey looked sideways at him, then nodded.

Soon they saw the gate and reined in toward the house.

It was nearing dusk, and it was good timing to stop for the night. No other reason, really, to have pulled in here, Brady told himself. Although he would admit, it would be interesting to see the little lady again.

She stepped out onto the porch as they neared. "Well, I'll be damned. You two again! Good to see you."

Brady tipped his hat. "You, too, ma'am. Wondering if we can spend the night here."

"Sure, sure. No trouble a'tall." She squinted into the gathering darkness. Where's your dog?"

"Oscar didn't make it."

"Oh. I'm sorry. He seemed like a fine dog."

"Yep."

"Go on over toward the barn, and I'll fix up some supper for you."

"Thanks, ma'am."

They turned their horses into the small corral, pumped water for them, laid out their bedrolls just inside the door of the barn, washed up slightly, and headed for the house.

Brady tapped at the door and opened it. Good smells inside.

"Well, it's lucky I had started this meal early today. And there's plenty. Chicken and dumplin's."

Brady and Harvey looked at each other, a little surprised.

"Thought you guarded your chickens pretty carefully," Brady said.

"Just the hens. The hens are special. The young cockerels get their necks wrung pretty regular."

The men sat at the little table, watched as the little lady finished dishing up the chicken and dumplings, the fried carrots, sliced bread. Glasses of cold milk were placed by each of them.

"Ma'am, this looks like a feast." It was true. Very different, but certainly a feast.

"My name's Olene. Gretchen Olene Ballard," she announced. "No need to call me 'ma'am'."

They ate, she chattered, asking about their travels, the weather where they'd been. Brady answered each of her questions briefly, careful not to speak with food in his mouth. Looking at her plate rather than at Brady, she asked if he was "married up."

"I was," Brady said quietly. Olene didn't pursue that topic, went on to ask about the railroad situation in Wyoming, the mining successes in the settlements, what they thought the weather might bring, where home was for Brady. Eventually she asked Harvey if he was married up.

"I have woman," Harvey answered solemnly. Brady wondered: Did Harvey indeed have a woman, or was he afraid the little lady was after him?

It was a fine meal. The weeks of jerky made the rich sauce of the chicken and dumplings even better. And apple pie! It was a dessert almost too good to be true. Harvey finished his pie, drank the last swallow of cold milk, then signaled that he'd go out to look after the horses. He nodded toward the little lady and said quietly, "Thank you, ma'am. Fine food."

The little lady began clearing the table. Brady stood close by and handed her glasses and plates. She was nearly through washing the dishes when he said, "I need to go help Harvey. But thank you for this fine meal."

"I'm proud to have you here." She wiped her hands on the dish towel. "I'm wondering. Will you do one thing for me?"

"Sure. What is it?"

She was nervous. "Please. Just ....could you please just give me a hug?"

It gave him a start.

"It don't have to mean anything much... just ...I'm glad you're here."

He moved awkwardly toward her, put his arms out. She stepped quickly into the embrace. She was so small! She can't weigh a hundred pounds, maybe not even ninety, he thought. But there was womanness to her. The top of her head could have fit under his arm; he smelled her soap, her shampoo. His chin rested gently on top of her curly hair. She moved even closer, slowly tightened her arms around his back.

"Thank you, Brady Quillan." Her voice was muffled against his chest and he felt her breath through his shirt. "You're a fine man." She stepped away, blew her hair off her forehead.

Brady swallowed, turned away, grabbed his hat and headed toward the door. "I'll just be goin' out, ma'am. We'll leave early in the morning. Thank you for a fine supper."

He clomped out the door, held it carefully so it didn't slam, and stepped off the porch. The horses were in the little corral with plenty of feed and water, and Harvey had removed their bedrolls from the packs. They looked around carefully to be sure they weren't in the way of any chickens. They'd never know which was "family" and which was the next meal for the little lady.

They slept well. The horses were quiet. Only a few coyotes howled. They awoke before the rooster crowed, but there was already a lantern lit in the little house. They had saddled up and were ready to leave when Olene came out with a small bundle. "I didn't want to hold you up with breakfast, so I just packed it for you." Harvey accepted the bundle. "It's eggs and bacon biscuits." She handed each of them a lidded jar. "Here's coffee. With cream and sugar. Be careful on your way." She smiled a quick little smile. "Maybe I'll see you again one of these days."

"Thank you for everything, ma'am. You sure have treated us well." Brady tipped his hat. Harvey nodded and lifted a hand in farewell.

Brady and Harvey moved out quickly, well rested and eager to make good progress. They both looked back toward the little lady as they passed through the gate.

Olene watched them go, and in her mind, she was making plans. She could sell this place. Her damn neighbor was always nagging her about buying it anyway. She'd buy a slightly bigger wagon. Load up two crates of chickens and feed. Her money bag. Her suitcase. With trousers, shirts, her underthings, those little black slippers and that blue dress. A nice nightgown. She'd hire somebody to go with her through the Badlands, then she'd be okay on her own the rest of the way. What would Brady Quillan think when she drove up to his place? Well, she'd handle that when the time came. He was a fine man. A fine man indeed.

Chapter 20

They rode steadily for several hours. Brady kept a lookout for a small settlement with a train station. It was his plan to avoid riding through the Badlands, move as quickly as they could toward Mount Alta, determine whether Harvey would stay there or continue on with Brady to his ranch. Brady didn't like the thought of leaving Harvey behind--he'd become accustomed to considering Harvey's opinion in nearly everything he did.

They finally came to the little town where the crooked sheriff had apparently tried to cash in on the bounty for Leon Norby. The little place didn't have much to offer, but there was a small train station there. Brady and Harvey had talked it over briefly, and Harvey agreed the train ride would be a good option. Brady made arrangements for their passage to Mount Alta, and after a couple of hours' wait, they were able to board. This time the horses were loaded into a cattle car and Harvey and Brady rode in a passenger car. At each stop, they checked on the horses, replenished water and hay. It was a long way, but the horses were traveling well. Harvey was traveling well, too, although he didn't close his eyes to rest. Food was offered to the passengers; both Brady and Harvey declined.

Several hours into their trip, Brady asked Harvey if he wanted to get off the train at Mount Alta. Harvey was quiet for a few moments. Then his solemn words came out. "I have people in many places. Some near your ranch by Sioux City. I will go with you that far." He nodded his head in agreement with his own words. "My people there. You are there. It is one. Same."

"That's good news to me, Harvey. You remember I have given you land there. You will always have a place with me."

The long train trip was tiring for the horses and for Brady and Harvey as well. But they did finally arrive at the little town near Sioux City that was closest to Brady's ranch. Even the air smelled fresher to Brady as they unloaded the horses. They saddled up, stowed the gear in the worn deerskins they'd used for the past several weeks, and headed out toward Brady's ranch. It was hard for Brady not to go at a gallop; how fine it would be to be back home!

It took them half a day. The sorrel seemed to realize, too, that they were near home. His ears pricked up, his gait quickened. Finally the gate to the place was there in front of them. Brady gulped down a lump in his throat; it was for Sullie, who was no longer there.

Tassle wasn't there; apparently he was over at the Marsh place. But things were in order in the house, and Brady showed Harvey a bed he could use. There was food in the kitchen. It felt strange here. Things seemed smaller, crowded. He seemed clumsy in his own house. It would take a while to become accustomed to being home again.

Harvey was silent. Brady walked with him to the corrals and barn, and they worked together to care for the horses and stow the packs in the barn. Tomorrow would come quickly. They'd round up Tassle, then ride the fences, check the cattle, settle in.

* * *

The next morning, Tassle rode in on Buck. He was surprised, delighted to see Brady back home. They had a warm greeting for each other, and Tassle was pleased to see Harvey. Harvey knew of Brady's confidence in Tassle, and he trusted the young man totally. He headed to the barn to brush the horses, leaving Brady and Tassle to catch up on ranch business. The place looked great; at a distance, the cattle looked great as well. Harvey could see that Tassle had done a good job.

"Tassle, this is a rough one. I don't think you could possibly know it, but Duke Marsh is dead." Brady swallowed hard. "And Cora is in jail." A pause. "And I don't think there's any way Dan could know this, either."

Tassle held up a hand. "No, Brady, you're wrong. The sheriff was out here some time ago and told Dan about that. Dan was upset for a while, of course, but he settled down. I've seen him many times, and he's always business-like and friendly.

There are no problems with him."

It was a big relief for Brady. He adjusted his hat, then said dryly, "That's good. We'll tell him to be sure not to move any fences."

Tassle mentioned, also, almost shyly, that he'd taken up with a girl from town who spent quite a bit of time with him at the other place. He hoped that was okay.

"Sure, no problem." He thought of himself and Sullie at the Marsh place. Maybe there was a magic there that would charm Tassle's connection with this girl.

Brady was eager to get back into the ranch routine. The weeks on the trail seemed a whole different life. He'd turn back into a rancher instead of a tracker. Harvey might find it a little hard to adjust, but they'd work it out.

* * *

Harvey and Brady had been home several weeks, had survived the cold winter, helped the new calves enter the world, worked some new horses, spent time with Tassle and Tassle's new woman, made repairs and improvements to buildings on both places. Made good progress. Probably the most satisfying improvement for Harvey was the construction of a small addition to the barn--a cabin, with an iron stove, a pump at the door, a built-in cot--although Harvey normally slept on the floor. He did have a fine buffalo robe for a rug, so it wasn't as cold or as hard as it might have been. He maintained a small fire pit just outside the cabin door, and the aroma of frybread was often in the air. He came into Brady's house often, cooked on the stove or fed the heating stove, but his cabin was his personal domain, and he took good care of it.

Harvey communicated in both his Indian English and his white man's English, depending on situation and mood. Often Brady would start a conversation by saying, "Remember when....". When Harvey started a conversation, it would be with a single word or two: "Train ride." Or "Badlands." "Richard." They spoke often of their adventures, the hard times and the easy times. They didn't speak often of Oscar. It was still too painful for both of them. Brady had mentioned chicken and dumplings a couple of times. But they didn't have chickens, so that wasn't on the menu.

Harvey had left two or three different times on long trips but always seemed to be glad to get back. And Old Horse never looked the worse for wear. He never looked good, but he never looked any worse. Brady didn't know where Harvey went on his times away, and Harvey never had visitors at the ranch. He was well liked in town, but there were no social connections there, as far as Brady could see.

It was late afternoon and they were putting new boards in the back of an old trailer they'd use to haul hay when the time came to mow. Suddenly Harvey straightened and looked to the west. "Wagon come."

Brady looked across the field to the road. There was still a little snow in the ditches. The sun was going down, and the wagon and its driver were silhouetted, dark against the golden sky. "Who the hell would that be?" He pushed his hat back on his head, squinted into the sunset. "And what the hell is in the back of that wagon? Looks like chicken crates or somethin'."

"Yes. Chicken crates," Harvey agreed.

The little lady drove right up to the gate, then hopped down, light as dandelion fluff. "Well, Brady Quillan, we meet again," she chirped. "And you, too, Harvey Two Shirts."

She moved toward them, hand outstretched. Brady took the hand, and she turned to shake with Harvey. Both men were stunned, not really able to speak. But the talking was done by the little lady.

"I had a good trip. No trouble a'tall. Your place is nice. Your stock looks good. Where can I unload my chickens? They'll need water right away." Without waiting for a reply, she moved to lift the wire crates out of her wagon. Harvey moved quickly to help. But Brady spoke up firmly. "Ma'am, you can't stay here. This is not a place for a woman. We're all men here." He looked at her, straight in the eye. "It wouldn't be fittin'."

Olene hesitated briefly. "We'll settle that. Meanwhile, these chickens need water." She bustled around, looking for a pump, then filled a small bucket and poured water into each cage.

"Hens are special critters. I like 'em to be fed and watered real regular."

Brady was determined--and almost threatened. "You can't stay here, ma'am."

She interrupted. "I'm Olene, not 'ma'am."

"Yes ma'am. Olene. You can't stay here. It's only men."

"You and me need to talk, Brady Quillan. Let's just sit on the porch here while I say some things." She bustled toward the porch where several chairs had been placed for late evening relaxation.

Harvey motioned that he would be in his lean-to and left hurriedly. Brady could have used the support but didn't stop him

Olene settled her little self in a big chair and started her lecture.

"Now Brady Quillan, you are a man alone. And you have no need to be alone." She tilted her head and looked at him. "I am a woman alone, and I don't need to be alone." She looked out across the yard. "You need help here in the house, I'm sure. I can do everything necessary in a house--I can clean, cook, do laundry." She puffed up a little. "I can garden, help in the field, muck out stalls, milk cows if you have any. I can nurse calves, help with branding, store up vegetables for the cellar."

Brady listened to each point. Olene didn't leave a second open for him to ask a question or to respond in any way. Using her fingers, she counted off more assets. "I can sew, mend clothes, and fences, too. I can mend hurt critters and humans, either one. I can sing a little and play a mouth harp. I can tell a story or wipe a fevered brow. I make a good companion."

She finally took a breath. And Brady was quick to take advantage.

"Ma'am, there is no place for a woman here. I am glad you'd want to be here. But there is NO PLACE FOR A WOMAN." He emphasized the words--louder and more slowly.

Brady took a breath, then continued, quietly. "You were kind to me and Harvey, and we appreciate that. But I gave my heart a while back, and I have no heart to give any more. And I don't want the responsibility of a woman. And I don't want a woman here for any reason."

Olene was stricken. But Brady was firm. "I'm sorry, ma'am. Olene. I'm sorry. But you gotta go."

He took a breath. "We'll feed you tonight. And then go with you to the neighbor's place. They're good people, and they have extra room, and there's a woman there." He rested then, relieved that he got it all out.

Olene didn't speak for a moment. Then, quietly, "It was a dream of mine that I had since I saw you." She gulped. "You are a fine man. A fine man." She picked at the fringe of her shawl. "I reckon I can understand what you're sayin'. But it's a big hurt. A real big hurt."

Brady rose, opened the door for her. "Come on in the kitchen and we'll eat. Then we'll go to the neighbor's. I think you'll find the man there a pretty fine man, too." Brady smiled to himself. "A fine man." Dan was in for a surprise. A big little surprise.

* * *

After the quick meal, Brady tied a horse to the back of Olene's wagon, helped her up into the spring seat, and they headed toward Dan's place. It didn't take long, and it was still light when they approached the main gate. Olene had paid close attention all the way. Now she straightened up in her seat. "My, this is a nice place. A fine place." She squinted to see livestock in the pasture. "Cattle look fine, too."

One of Dan's hands came up from the small house--a man Brady knew was married. He greeted the man smoothly. "Hello. I wanted to see Dan for a minute. Brought him some company."

"He's out in the pasture, be in real soon. Get on down and have a seat here in the yard. My wife'll be out in a minute. She'll be glad to have some visitors." He turned toward the corrals, lifting a hand to shade his eyes, apparently on the look-out for Dan.

Brady helped Olene down from the wagon. She looked carefully all around. Brady figured she wasn't missing a single detail. They sat on the wooden chairs in front of the larger house; it would be where Dan lived. Very soon a young lady approached from the smaller house, a big smile on her face.

"Hi, folks. Welcome! Brady, good to see you again." Then, turning to Olene, "I'm Helen Wagoner. So glad you're here." Olene didn't wait for Brady to introduce her. "I'm Gretchen Olene Ballard. Just call me Olene. From over toward the Black Hills." Brady winced as Olene started her babbling. "This is such a nice place. I've seen so many miles of good pasture, and there are fine-looking cattle around. I never did have many cattle, just a few. I mostly have chickens. I just love having chickens. Do you have any chickens?" Finally there was brief pause, as if she really expected a response. Helen had caught up with her chatter enough to answer. "Not recently. We used to." Then catching a movement just on the other side of the corral, "Oh, there's Dan!"

Olene looked quickly, then moved her head toward the figure, looked more intently. "A fine looking man. Fine looking man."

Brady spoke to Helen, quickly and seriously. "Helen, I thought maybe you would like the company of Olene for a while. I'm not really set up for company, and I know you have room. Maybe you have need for some help, too." Helen was nodding, a big smile on her face.

Brady continued. "I've gotta get back to my place before dark, so I won't wait for Dan to come up here to the house. But tell him I hope he's gettin' along okay and I'll see him soon." Brady tipped his hat. "Olene, ma'am, it was good to see you again. I'm sure we'll see you before long. Take good care of your chickens." He hurried toward the wagon to get his horse.

"Yes, Brady Quillan. Thank you for everything. You're a fine man." She turned back toward Helen, then turned her attention toward Dan Marsh. Yes, he looked like a fine man. A fine man indeed.

Epilogue

The years sped by. Brady and Harvey had begun a good breeding and training program for ranch horses, and Harvey proved to be as good a horseman as Brady. Harvey had begun developing a herd of his own cattle and added to it regularly with orphan calves, occasional purchases from the market in town, trades with neighboring ranchers for horse training or round-up work. He left fairly regularly for time away from the ranch; Brady never knew where he went. Olene of course stayed with Dan Marsh, functioning well as his boss lady and providing lively company for Helen. Even Dutch Heisler seemed to thrive under Olene's supervision. And there were plenty of chickens at Dan Marsh's place.

Brady never developed an attachment to another dog anywhere near as strong as the attachment he had to Oscar. And he never developed an interest in another woman. Sullie was his one and only love. She would never age in his memory. He lived to old age with the vision of her as his perfect companion. With time, his recollection of the violence in his pursuit of Duke Marsh faded, and in quiet, sunset moments, he again felt the peace and calm that came to him with the successful end he and Harvey Two Shirts had come to on their trail to justice.

Afterword

Only a very few Lakota words are used in this short novel. The pronunciation of these words is provided below, thanks to the work of Paul WarCloud (1930-1973), artist and linguist of Sisseton, South Dakota.

ahbanah - AH-bah-nah. calm
abahyehnah - AH-bah-yeh-nah. quiet
eyopehyah - e-YO-peh-yah. punish
haychaydu - HAY-chay-du. correct
washteh - wash-TEH or WASH-teh. good

Thanks to: Educators, artists, authors, and the film makers who have made the Old West known to all--some with remarkable historical accuracy and some with less accuracy but much enthusiasm; and to family and friends whose interest and support have made this project even more rewarding.

About the authors—

Two little old ladies in their eighties have collaborated on this short novel set in the Dakota and Wyoming Territories. Both have admiration and respect for the Old West, the Native American heritage, good horses and good dogs, and the incredible power of the printed word. Both were born and spent younger years in South Dakota. One ended up in North Carolina, the other in Oklahoma by way of Wyoming. Both read, ride, and remember—three valuable activities which contribute to the authenticity of Trail to Justice. The original plan was to write a short little dime-western-type booklet; but Brady Quillan, Oscar, and Harvey Two Shirts demanded a little more…evidence of the power of the written word.